This is a work of fiction. Names, characters, businesses, places, events and incidents are either the products of the author's imagination or used in a fictitious manner. Any resemblance to actual persons, living or dead, or actual events is purely coincidental.

Contents

Charles Island

Connecticut Extreme Horror

A. Sanford

Copyright Sept.24, 2016

Friday Oct. 26 th

06:12 Hours

Sixty-nine-year-old Helen Johnson is energetic. At the crack of dawn, she heads out of her seaside residence, dressed in her pink jogging suit and white orthopedic sneakers. Tootsie, her hyperactive Bichon Frise is already pulling at the leash.

A block away from the senior condo complex is one of Connecticut's most beautiful stretches of shoreline. Silver Sands beach has magnificent views of the Long Island Sound. A unique point of interest is Charles Island. It is a 14 acre densely-wooded bird sanctuary a half mile from the coast. Subject to the tide, a rocky sandbar offers periodic access to the landmass by foot. Over the centuries, many have drowned not respecting the rising waters and rip current that can overtake a person caught out on the tombolo.

At this moment, it is low tide and the sailboat named the Sea Joy has run aground on the land bar. It lists to the side at a forty-five-degree angle. All of the rigging, cables, and lines have been snapped. Radar, lights, and telecommunications equipment on the main mass are missing. There is a dead stillness except for the lapping of waves as the vessel is silhouetted against the rising glow on the horizon.

With her Bichon pulling and yapping, Helen starts out on her morning routine of traversing the boardwalk, plastic bag in hand to pick up her dog's droppings. There comes the angry squawking of seagulls as they swarm and peck at the figure stuck on top of theboat's mast. Helen is unsure of the reason for the birds' commotion. She and Tootsie go onto the beach. They head toward the distressed vessel stuck out on the sandbar. As Helen and Tootsie get closer and closer to the boat, rays of sun begin to illuminate the day.

Like a gruesome kebab, the decapitated body of a 50-year- old Caucasian male is impaled on top of the mast. He is naked. His huge belly is drooping. Maroon colored splatter has dried on his pasty white skin and is encrusted in his chest hair. The fiberglass hollow spar has rammed through his perineum and rectum, displaying and fracturing his pelvic girdle. Multiple internal organs are catastrophically pierced and crushed. The shaft travels from between his legs, through his lower abdomen and up into his thoracic cavity. Ragged skin and muscle hangs from the stump of his neck. Both hands are missing below the wrist. He also has been castrated, leaving behind a nubby pale penis and a torn flap of scrotum. Parts of the boat's white mast is streaked with blood and feces. Red smears of gore are on the deck and on the wheel house.

"Chr-Chr-Christ!" Helen stutters. Her little Bichon is crazed, barking and jumping. The leash gets tangled around the woman's ankle. There is an audible pop as she falls and breaks her hip on the sandbar's wet rocks.

Piercing shrieks of the gulls reverberate and grow louder. It is a frenzy of blood-stained beaks and white feathers. The birds are not used to having such a large carcass to feed upon.

Friday Oct. 26th
06:31 Hours

A few miles up from Silver Sands beach is a small Catholic parish. Father Joseph, who is originally from Abuja, is preparing for morning mass. It is the feast of Demetrius of Thessaloniki, patron saint of the crusades. In the somber quietness, the priest exits the sacristy and walks out onto the alter. There is a vibe of silent foreboding in the empty church. Dawn's early light is beginning to illuminate the stained glass windows but the interior is mostly dark. Father Joseph abruptly stops. The small door to the tabernacle is open. For a moment, Father Joseph thinks there has been a robbery but then he sees the gold communion chalice placed in the center of the holy table. A faint beam of light shines on the vessel from a side window. A few droplets of red blood dot the white linen that covers the table slab. The chalice is full of, things.

"What is happening here?" the priest asks aloud in a thick Nigerian accent.

He quickly takes a closer look at the gold metal cup. A human eyeball stares back nestled in a coil of epididymis on top of a fleshy heap. It is like a cherry crowning an ice-cream Sunday. The chalice is crammed with two mangled testicles and various severed fingers.

"OH GOD!" Father Joseph screams. He reels backward, stumbling down the stairs. There is the sound of flapping wings high overhead in the church rafters. A small snowy white egret glides down and lands on the alter table. The bird has flown here from Charles Island. Like a delicate piece of living origami, the little bird walks over to the chalice on its black spindly legs. With a quick poke of its pointy yellow beak, it snatches up a segment of pink epididymis and swallows it like a worm.

Friday Oct. 26th

06:42 Hours

A few miles away at the Milford green, well-dressed business people, briefcases in hand, make their way to the Metro North train station as part of the early morning commute to Manhattan. Various old protestant places of worship stand proudly nearby. Elegantly landscaped parks and duck ponds adorn the area. It is quintessential Connecticut.

The First Congregation church has the highest steeple. It is there that the severed head of the man from the boat is stuck on top of the spire. A lifeless eye-ball stares out over the rooftops and distant tree line. The other eye socket is gouged out and empty. Both ears have been removed along with the tongue and left far down below in a little pile on the doorstep of the adjunct Bible study center. Initially, no one notices the mortal remains. It is the beginning of a crisp autumn day with bright blue skies. A pigeon flies over and roosts for a moment on the decapitated head. The bird then flaps away in a startled panic, shitting on top of the head as it goes. Far in the distance toward the shoreline, the first emergency sirens can be heard.

Friday Oct. 26th
06:55 Hours

Marsha had planned to get up earlier to do yoga but drank too much Zinfandel and popped one too many Xanax the night before. The sound of ambulance sirens wakes her out of her grogginess. She is alone in bed on the top floor of the old seaside house overlooking the beach. The rising sun shines through the large bay window and hurts her eyes.

"Oh please," Marsha mutters. "Not another fucking migraine." Rubbing her temples, she becomes more alert. Black mascara streaks her cheeks. Marsha is unaware that she had been crying while she dreamt. Wrapping a blanket around her naked body, she stands up and shivers. Marsha is tall and slim, with a small tattoo of a white egret on her left shoulder blade. Walking up to the bay window, she looks through the murky pane. Thin cracks zigzag the glass. A police officer in a SUV has driven out on Silver Sands beach. In the distance and off to the right, early morning joggers and dog-walkers have gathered out on the tombolo near the disabled vessel.

"What's wrong with that boat?" she gasps. "I hope that's not the one that Crystal is on."

Crystal is Masha's twin sister. They recently turned 27 and inherited their aunt's waterfront home. Both had attempted modeling when they were younger. Coming from NYC, Milford is bit of a bore. The two have done their best to amuse themselves with the local nightlife. It was there at one of the bars that Crystal met a middle aged man. He was a hedge fund manager that was into sailing.

Searching for her iPhone, Marsha calls her sister. It goes right to voicemail. Marsha leaves a message with a mixed tone of humor and anxiety. "Hello! Where are you? You didn't call me last night. I have a pounding fucking headache. I'm looking out the window at a fucked-up boat. It better not be you on there. Call me! And please don't let me believe that you are actually sleeping with that guy. Girl, you have an inheritance now, you don't have to blow ugly rich dudes anymore! Call me, bitch."

The sirens are growing louder as more emergency vehicles show up on the scene. Commercial fishing boats are approaching from the Long Island Sound. The Coast Guard has been alerted.

Marsha experiences an attack of the willies that makes her back muscles quiver. It is a familiar sensation. Many summers she spent here as a child with her sister. The happy times down at the beach were often ruined by night terrors and bouts of sleepwalking.

"I hate this place," Marsha says aloud as she clutches the blanket tighter around her body. Despite the test of time and numerous hurricanes, the house has survived. Its grey weathered exterior is missing many of its cedar shingles and the roof leaks. Black mold stains the sagging faded wallpaper and infuses the air with the stench of mildew and decay. Its field stone foundation dates back to the 1600's, the time of the first white European settlers in Milford. The sisters plan to have the house demolished and replaced with something bright and modern.

As Marsha walks across the ancient plank floor, the creaking wood is piercing. She stops in her tracks. Faint tapping could be heard down below in the cellar.

"Is someone there? Hello?" Marsha blurts out with fear in her voice.

There is no answer.

The tapping ceases, followed by unnerving silence.

Friday Oct. 26th

07:00 Hours

Phillip knows that he needs to get in the hole soon. The sun is out and he can be easily spotted. Since last night, he has been standing on the shore of Charles Island and witnessing the whole occurrence. An unseasonably warm bout has caused a blooming of mosquitos and sand fleas. His clammy, white skin is dotted with pink bumps. A Zika infected insect bite has swollen like a small tumor squarely in the center of his forehead. The temperature has since dropped in the morning hours. He now shivers. His black t-shirt and black jeans are damp. Mud coats his black Converse sneakers. His black bowl haircut is moist and plastered to his skull. Philip has just turned 16-years-old. He is short and paunchy but his wild blue eyes have a ferocious glint.

Gazing out at his unmanned orange kayak floating aimlessly in the surf, Phillip grins. Mom, must be really freaking out by now. Calling the school principle. Calling the police. Calling my therapist. I missed my chance to use my fucking sweet, bad-ass tanto! I should have gutted her before I took off yesterday. Imagine how they'd shit themselves if they found her head propped up in the middle of the coffee table.

Phillip stares back at the Sea Joy beached on the sandbar. More firefighters and police officers are clamoring onto the sailboat. The first responders are aghast as they inspect the impaled body on the mast.

"You guys don't know what you're in for!" Phillip laughs aloud.

A Coast Guard vessel races into the area. Instantly, Phillip is alarmed as it travels close to the side of the shore where he is standing. Charles Island's terrain is rocky with the interior covered with thickets of storm-battered hardwood trees. In a clumsy run, Phillip starts to flee the shore, tripping on mounds of seashells and wet sand. He makes his way up an embankment and reaches a plateau. He is now at the edge of the scraggly forest. Ducking down behind a bramble of felled branches, Philip waits. A few yards away is a crumbling stone and brick arch. It is 13 feet high and tagged with graffiti. It is one of the last remnants of an old Aquinas chapel from the 1930's. There is a freshly dug hole at the foot of the ruins. The opening in the ground is just big enough to accommodate Phillip's body. Phillip scampers headfirst into the hole like a large rodent escaping into its nest.

Friday Oct. 26th

12:00 Hours

It is now high tide and a salvage vessel equipped with a crane is assisting with the operation. A large canvas tarp has been hoisted up on the deck of the Sea Joy to block the view of the spectators and news media gathering on the shore. A forensic team dressed in their polyethylene Tyvek suits has besieged the boat and is handling the crime scene. They decide to remove the body by bisecting a section of the boat's mast. There is the sound of a hydraulic circular saw as it cuts through the aluminum alloy spar. Members of the forensic team awkwardly lower the corpse down and place it into a body bag. Approximately a meter of the impaling mast is left in the torso to be removed later during the autopsy.

Connecticut's State Homicide division has commandeered a rental cottage on the beach as an emergency command center. The place is packed with law enforcement personnel. Through the back window, there is a clear view of Charles Island. Town maps, schematics, and crime scene photos have been tacked up on the walls of the cottage.

Detective Helminski enters into the crowded room. He is 49 years old with a beer gut and a wrinkled sports jacket. He quickly catches the looks of disdain from some of the cops. His reputation of being a callous prick is true. Many know he is a drunk. Helminski addresses Brown, the lead coordinating commander, "To give you an update, we are checking all store and bank surveillance cameras. The fire department has a ladder crew removing the cabeza from the church steeple. It's a fucking clown show down there on the Milford green."

"Any theories on how the head got all the way up there?" asks Brown.

"Who the fuck knows," replies Helminski. "Maybe someone rigged it to a drone."

"Any ISIS flags draped about?" "Nothing like that yet."

"What else you got?"

"I just got report that a woman is saying her sister was on that boat."

"Where is she?"

"She's with local PD down at the Milford station. Her name is Marsha Stowe. She got arrested this morning for interfering with the crime scene. Supposedly, she was trying to get on board to find her sister. The chick got aggressive and smacked a trooper."

Brown sucks his teeth and replies, "Dive teams are searching the waters around the boat."

Helminski says, "An hour ago, I interviewed the Nigerian Priest. He was trembling so hard I thought he was going to pop an aneurysm. He literally crapped his pants. The boys from Homeland Security are chatting with him now. I'm on my way to go see Miss Marsha. I hope she's got better bowel control than the Padre."

In the next moment, a blood-speckled seagull flies into the back window of the commandeered cottage. The loud bang makes all the cops jump. A spider glass break destroys the sturdy storm pane. Outside on the ground, the stunned bird quivers in the sand. It dies from a broken neck.

Friday Oct. 26th

12:20 Hours

Helminski enters the lobby of the Milford Police Department. There is pandemonium. A man, originally from New Delhi, is crying aloud; the front of his white shirt is soaked with blood. His nose has been busted. Sari-clad relatives are gathered around sobbing and shrieking. The desk sergeant is overwhelmed with reporters and the surge of people coming into the precinct in a state of crisis.

"I am a victim of a hate crime!" shouts the Indian man. "A hooligan came into my FoodMart; called me a terrorist, and beat me in front of my wife! I am Hindu! Not Muslim! I did not desecrate the Christian churches with the body parts of the dead!"

A haggard, emaciated woman with greying hair, pushes through the crowd and comes up to the counter. There is the smell of cheap vodka on her breathe. She yells at the desk sergeant, "Hell with these goddam foreigners! My son is missing! He's my only boy! Ya gotta go find my little Phillip!"

Simultaneously, local reporters are barraging the old cop with questions.

Flashing his badge, Helminski is seen on the security camera and is buzzed through a side door. He proceeds to the restricted back area of the police department. The sound of shouting from the lobby murmurs through the walls.

"I'm here to question Marsha Stowe," Helminski says to the precinct captain.

"She's on a PTA. We cut her loose."

"Why the fuck did you do that?" Helminski fumes.

"We're stretched too thin! You can plainly see we got more important shit to handle in this town!"

"I need her address."

"I think the file is still on the table in the records office. She bolted out of here and left all her belongings. Looked like she was chased by a ghost."

Helminski does an about face and walks into the small unoccupied file room. The door closes shut on its own and there is a vacuum of unexpected silence. Positioned squarely in the middle of the table, is Marsha Stowe's file and a manila envelope containing her keys and iPhone. Helminski quickly skims the police report and jots down her address on a notepad. The iPhone vibrates in the envelope accompanied by a loud ringtone. It's a snippet of techno dance music. Helminski tears open the the manila envelope and retrieves the phone. An instantaneous jolt of panic makes him hesitate.

"Woah, what's that feeling? That's goddamn weird."

He waits until the fourth ring to accept the incoming call.

His words get stuck in his throat.

"Hi Marsha, it's me. Hello."

The female voice sounds distant and muffled.

Helminski is oddly mute for another moment. His heart is starting to pound.

"Hello? Are you there, Marsha?" asks the female voice.

Forcing a dry swallow, the detective regains his ability to speak. He stammers, "Ah, I have Marsha's phone at the moment."

"Okay, no problem," says the voice. "Can you please tell Marsha that this is her twin sister Crystal calling from under the island.

"Under the Island?"

"Yes, from under Charles's Island." Helminski then hears hissing on the other end.

The female voice says, "And can you also relay the message to Marsha, that the next time she sees me, I'm going to kill her."

The iPhone goes dead.

Helminski instantly feels his own bowels churn.

Friday Oct. 26th

12:55 Hours

Being in the holding cell had triggered an episode of catastrophic claustrophobia.

Marsha almost got hit by a truck when she initially fled the precinct and blindly bounded across double lanes of traffic on the Boston Post Road. The Milford police department is three miles inland from the shore. In the past, Marsha had been addicted to running which was fueled by her eating disorder. She had placed well in many races including the New York Marathon, but today is her best time ever. Her yellow tank top and pink yoga pants are drenched with sweat as she speeds down residential side streets in a crazed panic. Both flip-flops have flown off and she runs barefoot on the pavement. The pain coming from the bleeding soles of her feet does not register in Marsha's mind. Her only thought is to escape.

At this moment, the scent of saltwater is increasing in the air.

She is getting closer and closer to the shoreline. She takes a corner. Orange cones and yellow police tape block the street. With huge strides, Marsha diverts across a neighbor's yard and continues on. A Mini Cooper is parked in front of the old beach house. Her impulsive plan is to jump into her car and drive far away. Only when she reaches the vehicle does she finally realize that she left her car keys back at the police station.

"Fuck!" Marsha cries aloud with a heaving gasp.

She then notices the front door of the beach house is wide open. The three story sagging edifice looms tall and silent in front of her. Beckoning. Marsha battles with herself. I can't go back in there! I can't! I know it! But there is another set of keys upstairs in my bag! Fuck! What do I do?

At that second, she remembers the bottle of Xanax that is also in her pocketbook. The thought of popping a bunch of xany bars trumps paranoia. Marsha quickly moves along the pathway, hurdles the crumbling stone steps and disappears into the doorway of the residence.

The temperature in the foyer is abnormally frigid. It is a drastic contrast to the outside warmth of the day. Marsha automatically shudders but she continues pounding up the creaking, dark wood staircase. In very little time, she makes it to the third floor. There is a scant moment of relief as she spies her pocketbook on top of the dresser. She even pauses for a moment to cram a few clothing items into her bag.

From downstairs on the first floor comes a voice. It asks, "Hey, Marsha is that you up there?"

Marsha is jolted. "Crystal?"

With a mocking tone, the voice says, "At first you go looking for me. Now you want to abandon me. That's not very nice."

Trembling, Marsha cries in a high pitched squeal. "Crystal! Is that really you? Oh my God, where have you been?"

The voice says, "A man has your cell phone. Did he give you my message?"

An internal sense of dread warns Marsha not to go downstairs. Years of childhood nightmares were all premonitions of the horror she is about to experience. Her protective intuition is overridden. Marsha finds herself running down the stairs, hoping to hug her beloved twin sister. What was once Crystal is now standing in the foyer. The dank air is even colder. Making it to the bottom step, Marsha screams only for a split second before her thumping heart goes into atrial fibrillation and she pisses her pink yoga pants.

Friday Oct. 26th

13:20 Hours

Helminski has the psychological ability not to crack up when witnessing death. He never lost his nerve at a crime scene. Sadness and despair are masked by gallows humor. This talent makes him a good homicide detective. However, today his armor of emotional detachment will be pierced. Gut instinct tells him not to go to the Stowe residence alone but he finds himself solo in his blue Chevy Caprice. There is panic and excitement in the air. He could see it in people's faces as he passes through town on the way to the shoreline. The schools are in lock-down. Media is everywhere.

The Caprice pulls up next to the Mini Cooper parked in front of the old three story beach house. Helminski turns off his GPS on his phone and exits the car. He observes the front door of the residence is wide open. There is a peculiar stillness. The other beach homes on the street appear vacant. Upon approaching the entrance, Helminski quickly knocks a few times on the paint-peeling door jam and announces himself.

"Hello, it's Detective Helminski, state special crime squad.

May I come in?"

The foyer of the house is dark. Silent. Helminski feels a cold current of air. He shivers and enters the residence. The stench is instantly familiar to the detective. There is a nauseating mix of bodily fluids and excrement. Reflexively, Helminski whips the right bottom of his sport's jacket to the rear, to have clear access to his firearm. He does not draw yet.

"Is anyone home?

This is the police! I am in the house!

Please answer me!"

The detective's voice is authoritative but cannot mask his apprehension.

A breeze from the shore causes the sound of distant wind chimes. Helminski's pulse is pounding in his ears. He cautiously moves from the foyer, down a small dark hallway and to the living room.

"Fuck!" Helminski gasps as he quickly pulls out his compact Glock model 30.

Copious amounts of wet crimson are splattered on the faded floral wall paper. A lamp, end table, and wicker beach furniture have been toppled over. In the middle of the wood plank floor, is the lower half of a human body. It is clad in blood-soaked pink yoga pants. Both legs have been dislocated from the pelvis and have multiple fractures. The limbs are splayed out at odd angles. Slippery coils of intestines have been yanked out from the lower abdomen and left on the rug. A mangled human forearm has been flung up on top of the fireplace mantel.

Logically, Helminski should instantly call for back up but he freezes. Trancelike, his gaze follows the red smears across the living room floor to the adjoining porch. He also notices the bloody footprints. The back door leading out to the beach is open. Again, far-off wind chimes ting and ding from a neighbor's veranda.

Robotically, Helminski walks forward, following the blood trail. He almost falls on his ass as he steps and slips on what appears to be a kidney. There is the stench of salt air and perforated bowels.

The expression on the detective's face is suddenly flat and constricted but inside his mind, he is screaming at himself, What the fuck am I doing? Don't go out there! What's got hold of me?

With his will hijacked, Helminski proceeds out to the rear of the old house and on to the private stretch of shoreline. In the distance and off to the right, Charles Island is in view. Coast guard and dive team vessels can be seen encircled around the doomed sailboat. In front of the detective, the blood trail continues on across the beach. The upper half of the torso lays discarded midway as a sand encrusted grisly hunk. Nearing the surf, a tall blonde female is walking nonchalantly and carrying Marsha's decapitated head by the hair. The blonde woman is naked and streaked with gore. She suddenly stops, turns around and flashes a huge smile at the detective. With the bright blue sky, calm water, and pretty beach, there is an incongruent vibe as if she is frolicking at a seaside resort.

She calls out to Helminski with a laughing lilt in her voice, "I pulled Marsha apart like a piece of boiled chicken! The meat just came right off the bone!"

The detective continues to stand, hypnotized and unable to turn away from the nightmare scene.

"I'm Crystal!" the girl shouts. "Are you that guy that has my sister's cellphone? How come you didn't give Marsha my message? She was so surprised when she saw me."

The speed of the wind chimes, its urgency increasing.

Rocketing blood pressure and a hammering heart beat continues to accelerate inside the detective's body.

"Here catch!" Crystal yells playfully as she swings the decapitated head by the ponytail then lets it go like a ball on a tether. Marsha's head flies through the air, lands, and rolls toward Helminski. The detective stares down at the bloody remains at his feet. Avulsions have removed most of the facial features.

"Aw, don't feel bad," Crystal mocks. "Modelling days are over with. How's your PTSD doing at this moment?"

Both of Crystal's irises are shiny rings of yellow with red pupils. In contrast, her sclera is black like the ink of a squid. She says, "Listen, can you hurry up and go do that, thing."

There is a pause. Even though Crystal is down near the surf, her voice is piercingly clear in the detective's ears.

Helminski then stutters, "Th-th-thing?"

Crystal becomes impatient. "Don't be coy, you sad, awful man. You know what thing. It's that thing you always think about on Saturday nights when you are all alone in your apartment. Drinking until you're shit-faced. Crying like a little bitch."

The detective hears her words. A tear suddenly appears in his right tear duct and rolls down his cheek. He gives a nod of resignation and brings the muzzle of the Glock to his temple and pulls the trigger. A brass shell casing flips into the air and briefly flashes with a glint of sunshine. The sudden cranial pressure causes his right eyeball to bulge out of its socket like a startled cartoon character. With a rapid jerk of his head and a quick spurt of blood from the entry wound, the .45 caliber hollow-point passes through

Helminski's brain but does not fully exit. The expanded bullet winds up on the opposite side of his skull as a lump under his scalp.

Soiling his beige trousers as he falls, the sound of the gunshot echoes down the beach and out across the water.

Friday Oct. 26th

14:05 Hours

Auxiliary Constable John Buck is standing on the embankment of Charles Island near the old ruins. He just heard the distant gunshot echoing from the shore. He knowingly smiles. A foot away, Phillip's moon-shaped face can be seen, peering skyward from his tight hole in the ground. The boy's chubby white cheeks are smeared with earth. Grotesquely, the mosquito bite in the middle of his forehead has grown larger. Phillip spits outs some pebbles and giggles.

John Buck addresses the boy, "You have a mischievous nature, son. Its okay, I was naughty too as a youngster. They tried to send me here to pray. The island was once a spiritual retreat for unruly juveniles. Hurricanes upon hurricanes over the years put a stop to all that mind control." Patting the grey crumbling mortar on the archway, Buck gloats, "No chapel is allowed here anymore. See this archway and those few piles of bricks over there? That is all that remains of the intrusion. These ruins are a testament to the authoritarian's defeat."

Sounds of rustling can be heard.

In haste, Buck quickly whispers, "Enjoyed chatting with you, son, but let me cover you back up. I think another patrol is coming through the woods."

Phillip squeals with delight, as if he is playing a game with a kindly old grandfather. Buck is wearing green Mucks, size extra-large. Buck places his muddy rubber boot on the teenager's up turned face. He steps down firmly and warns. "Stay deep in your hole, son. Don't let them see you until it's time."

Sounds of sputtering and choking can be heard. Buck then kicks some nearby twigs and dead sea grass over the opening for concealment.

A few moments later, two federal agents come bursting through the forest and out onto the embankment. They are young, jacked, and dressed in black tactical fatigues. Both are armed with Colt M4s. In contrast, Auxiliary Constable Buck is over seventy, gray haired, tall and lumbering. His old blue uniform shirt is stained with coffee and he carries a revolver in a well-worn leather holster. Despite his age, he has a strange manic vitality.

Jovially, John Buck calls out to the young men, "Better check yourself for ticks. Lyme Disease is rampant this year. See any deer in the interior?"

Agent Ortiz ignores the question and address Buck in a hostile tone. "You were ordered by the last patrol to vacate this area. You are not a full active duty officer. Your only assignment is to be directing traffic in town. You are not allowed to be on this island."

Buck glares with a bitter smile and asks, "Does a policeman ever retire? Where are you boys from?"

Agent Miller responds, "We are agents from the special response team from the Department of Homeland Security. This island is now under our jurisdiction."

Buck smirks. "Homeland Security? I guess you two hot shots

are on the look out for Jihadists. There are no Osama bin Ladens here. You are barking up the wrong tree. My heritage goes back to the first settlers in Milford. This island has my soul. I know what is really happening. The truth is a trillion times more catastrophic then a terrorist act. I assure you."

"We are not here to discuss the matter with you," snaps Ortiz. "Walk around to the west side of the island and take a police vessel back to shore."

Abruptly, Buck drops his smile and stares at the agents with frigid intensity. Buck asks them, "Do you two like to collect seashells? Do you? Did you ever hear the disrespectful phrase, go pound sand up your ass? You will soon experience it in a literal sense."

"Are you threatening us?" snares, Ortiz.

There comes the sound of splashing near the shore. Buck turns around, raises his hands and instantly beams with delight.

"Who are you signaling?!" barks Agent Miller.

Buck returns his attention back to the two agents and replies, "Signaling? I wasn't signaling anyone. I was just waving at Crystal. She was swimming by. She just disappeared under the water again. My gosh, what a beauty!"

"Crystal?" asks Ortiz.

"Yes, Crystal," Buck swoons. "She's lovely, like a mermaid. Don't worry, you'll meet her."

Friday Oct. 26 th

17:01 Hours

On deck of the Coast Guard cutter, the commanding officer is feeling a growing sense of danger. He was made aware of an "officer down" incident that occurred not too far from his present location offshore. At this time, a final dive is being conducted before the Sea Joy is towed off the sandbar and brought to dry dock.

Ten minutes passed and a new surge of alarm hits the crew as communication is lost with one of the two rescue divers. Surface marker buoys start to drift aimlessly about in the water. The leads have been cut. One of the rescue divers unexpectedly bursts to the surface in distress. He is quickly hoisted up on deck. Pulling off his diving mask, he starts screaming and gagging, "Porto is missing! Our buddy-line got severed. Someone else is swimming around down there!"

Other crewmembers try to calm the man down.

He cries, "The visibility sucked, I dropped a strobe. I only saw her for a second in the flash! You got to go find Porto! I think she took him!"

The man then goes into cardiac arrest and dies despite the crew's frantic efforts to save his life.

Friday Oct. 26th

23:11 Hours

Near the Devon community of Milford, a small raised ranch is on fire. The front bay window explodes from the searing heat, allowing tongues of flames to flicker out toward the roof. Inside the residence, meek high-pitched cries of agony abruptly stop. A few elderly neighbors watch from across the street and are aghast. Auxiliary Constable John Buck is standing in the front yard of his home with an empty five-gallon gas can at his feet. He has soaked himself head to toe with petrol. Flying hot embers are coming dangerously close to igniting his body but he remains calm despite the stinging in his eyes and the periodic reflex to cough and gag from the fumes. He is still wearing his old police uniform. The Ruger Security Six is holstered on his hip. A red road flare is tightly grasped in his left hand. Resolute, Buck awaits and listens to the approaching sirens.

The town's emergency response teams have been stressed to the max with chaos of the day. A huge turntable ladder rig arrives along with an ambulance before the local police. All of the firemen know Auxiliary Constable John Buck and they initially rush forward to help but are soon baffled as they see him draw his revolver with his free hand. Many in the department considered Buck an oddball and often talked behind his back regarding his mental stability. Buck takes a wild shot at their vehicle. The .38 caliber wad-cutter shatters a side mirror on the truck.

"What the hell?" shouts one of the firemen as he cringes.

Others hit the dirt.

Buck spits to clear his irritated throat, then says with a rasp, "You fellas, hold your horses. Lives won't be saved anymore." His labored words are indiscernible in the clamor of crackling flames.

"John! what are ya doing?" Yells one of the paramedics. "Put down the goddamn gun!"

With a crazed glare, Buck mutters to himself, "Never in my entire life, have I ever been so humiliated like today. Those government thugs rudely escorted me off my beloved island like I was some vagrant!"

"Where's your wife, Betty, John? Is she okay?"

Betty had been crippled with the final stages of Parkinson's disease. Buck had left her handcuffed to her wheelchair when he set their house ablaze.

Buck coughs then says, "I sacrificed my wife's life tonight to honor Charles Island."

With the flashing of red and blue lights, finally a local squad car arrives. Quickly, Buck holsters his revolver and uncaps the road flare. In a hurry, his coordination is poor. He fails to get an ignition strike in the first three attempts.

One of the firemen shouts to the cop emerging from his police cruiser, "Careful, this senile bastard just took a shot at us!"

On the fourth scrape, Buck manages to light the road flare. He coughs one last time and proclaims, "I now sacrifice myself. All of you, go pound sand up your ass! I regret I will not be around when the island blooms."

They witness Auxiliary Constable John Buck taking the sparking flare and placing it under his chin. In a flash, his head is aglow in a dazzling pink light. His gasoline-soaked body bursts into flames. Buck manages to run halfway across the lawn in a frenzied charge before collapsing. His fiery hulk writhes on the ground. The firemen do not attempt to douse the burning man with their extinguishers. They all freeze instead. A sudden strange force blocks every single emergency responder from giving any kind of aid. For a long grueling stretch of time, they observe the immolation in an unholy silence. Turning onto his back, Buck's legs bend up and his arms constrict into partial flexion. His mop of white hair has been scorched away. His head is now bald and smoldering. Retracted, blackened lips give rise to a skeletal grin. A few .38 wad-cutters cook off and bulge in the cylinder of the white-hot Ruger Security Six revolver. Melted abdominal tallow has fused with the charred thick leather of his old gun belt. Sweet and meaty odors of a roasted corpse wafts into the night air.

With the passing of a few more minutes, the roof of the raised ranch caves in, followed by a burst of bright orange and bellowing black smoke. Nearby trees are starting to catch fire. The emergency responders continue to stare motionless. They are perplexed and terrified by their inability to react. All are made reverent to the inferno.

Sunday Oct. 28th

13:16 Hours

"I'm so jealous!" Courtney exclaims with excitement. "Do you see how much media attention there is! Milford has made national news! I gotta be part of this! What angle should we go with? Captain Kidd's ghost? The curse of the Aztec gold? Indian spirits? You can see what I'm partial to. How cute do I look in this outfit? Tell me, do I look hot?"

Courtney is dressed in a Halloween pirate costume that she bought at a porno combo lingerie shop. Her long straight blonde hair hangs down from under her purple head scarf. She is adorned with a black eye patch, red sash, and knee high leather boots. The three others in cramped downtown Milford apartment look at her and have varied reactions.

Blowing out a cloud of pot smoke, Ed gives a dirty grin and says, "You look like a stripper. You're over 18, right?"

"I'm 21!" Courtney snaps back.

Ed is almost thirty and is going nowhere in life. He recently got out of jail again for larceny. He is tall, lanky and sunburned. Both of his sinewy forearms are marred with crude tattoos. The green blotchy prison art was created with pricks from dirty needles. Ed does not know about his diagnosis Hepatitis C. Working part time on local fishing boats, he does know a thing or two about the waters of the Long Island Sound.

"Tell your brother, thanks for recommending me for this job," says Ed. "How's he doing?"

"He's in rehab," replies Courtney.

Ed nods knowingly and says, "When he gets out, make sure he looks me up right away. I know where to score some primo Fentanyl."

Jason cuts in and states flatty, "Courtney, I don't understand why you are dressed like that."

Courtney met Jason in college. They were both communication majors. She considers Jason a weirdo. His diagnosis of Asperger's Autism is beyond her level of comprehension and compassion. The one thing she does value about Jason is his filming and technology skills.

"You are such a nerd, Jason," Courtney scolds. "You'll never understand show business. We need to be different. Have some fun! All these reporters on TV are so-o-o-o serious! I need people to look at me. Everybody loves Pirates of the Caribbean."

Jason stares back at Courtney, void of affect. His large coke bottle glasses make his gray eyes appear large and distorted. Jason's attention then returns back to all the video recording components laid out on the linoleum floor. Systematically, he starts rechecking the equipment.

"We can't take this lightly," Ruth warns. "People have been murdered. There have been unexplained suicides. Others are missing. Negative forces have besieged this plane of reality. My cat is having nightmares."

"Really, your cat is freaking out?" Ed says with a laugh. "Yes, both me and my cat are clairvoyant," replies Ruth sternly.

"Damn, real psychics?" Ed mocks. "Can you and your pussy predict six Power Ball numbers for me?"

Ruth ignores Ed's question and reflexively clutches the small silver pentagram hanging from a chain around her neck. She sits uncomfortably in the beer stained couch. Her morbid obesity often affects her breathing. Dressed in a XXL black t-shirt and bulging black jeans, her thick black eye mascara, black fingernail polish and magenta hair, completes her Neo-Wiccan image.

"Listen, I don't want to concentrate on anything too dark," says Courtney. "The plan is, I'll host the pod cast and interview Ruth. She'll go into a trance and try to contact the ghost of Captain Kidd. We'll make it kind of light hearted and quirky. I like romantic vampire stuff, nothing too scary."

Ed responds gruffly, "You do know that body parts have been left around town, right?"

"Yuck, gross!" Courtney shudders. "Let's not go there." "Well, how close do you want to get to the island?" Ed asks.

Courtney replies, "I need you to row us out just far enough for Jason to launch his video drone. We'll record some aerial shots of the woods and beach. I'm envisioning shaky camera angles, murky green infrared. The whole time I'll be narrating. Then we'll cut back to Ruth and she can start her talking-to-the-dead shtick."

Ruth scowls and says, "It's not a shtick. When I start channeling, it is very real."

Feigning an apology, Courtney says, "Oh, I'm so sorry Ruth. I really value political correctness. I want to say, I truly respect your paranormal views."

Courtney first learned about Ruth from a flyer tacked up on the wall of a local coffee shop. Ruth was advertising $20 dollar psychic readings and love spells.

Ed takes another hit from his blunt and squints at Ruth with pink eyes. Cruelly he says, "Are you sure you can handle the trip?"

Ruth knows he is referring to her weight and she replies, "How wide is your boat and how strong can you row?"

Ed laughs and shakes his head, "It can get choppy out there on the water."

Jason asks, "Will I get motion sickness?"

"You better not, Jason!" Courtney says. "I need you to do your job and not be such a wimp. Our podcast can go instantly viral! We can be a YouTube overnight sensation! My goal is a million 'likes!'"

Sunday Oct. 28th

22:31 Hours

A low-lying fog masked their launch from Silver Sands Beach. The old rowboat is 17 feet long. It is shoddy with peeling paint and barely seaworthy. One of the wooden benches has been removed to allow Ruth to squeeze in near the bow. Courtney and Jason are presently seated in the middle while Ed is aft, straining with the oars.

A half a mile away, blinking blue and red emergency lights illuminate the mist. Coast Guard vessels remain positioned near Charles Island. Authorities continue to frantically search for Porto, the missing rescue diver. The nearby shoreline and surrounding waters have been deemed ever-broadening, active crime scenes.

Ed grunts as he rows. 50 minutes pass. Enduring choppy waves, they make it around to the outer side of the island. Obsessively, Jason wipes off moisture droplets from his digital video equipment. The electronic gear is partially protected under a tarp. Jason asks aloud, "Statistically, what are the chances that we'll be arrested for being out here?"

"Fuck the po po!" Ed curses. "They won't be able to spot shit!"

"The fog is dense," affirms Jason.

Ed asks, "Okay nerd boy, we've been out here for a while. Are we close enough yet for your little toy airplane?"

"It's not a toy airplane," Jason replies. "It is a state of the art cinematic drone. And yes, I believe we are in range."

"Good, cause my shoulders are fucking killing me." Ed immediately stops rowing. The water looks pitch black in contrast with the gray drifting mist. Unseasonably high humidity combines with a heavy stench of salt air and algae.

Embarrassed, Courtney dabs her chin again with pink tissues from her make up bag. A little earlier, she threw-up partially digested segments of a protein bar mixed with a geyser of organic Kombucha.

Ed snickers and teases Courtney, "Sure you're okay little sister? I thought pirates don't get seasick!"

Courtney glares back at Ed, "If you tell anybody I puked, I won't pay you a dime!"

"Aye, aye skipper!" Ed laughs. "Your secret is safe with me! How's Broom Hilda doing there at the bow?"

Ruth also appears pale and green with motion sickness. Her wheezing is loud and disturbing. She gasps, "I-I forgot my inhaler."

"What? You didn't predict that?" Ed says sarcastically. "You can't afford to have an asthma attack out here on the water. It's really dark tonight. Almost the witching hour. If you croak, who will take care of your cat?"

Aggravated, Courtney snaps at Ed, "Leave her alone; she'll be fine!" Courtney then addresses Jason. "Let's do this! Jason, are you ready? Do we have a connection out here?"

"Sort of," Jason replies as he fiddles with his laptop. "It's spotty."

Courtney takes a deep breath and tries to ease her transitory nausea. Her pirate costume is damp from the ocean spray. Black mascara has run down her cheeks. Adjusting her eye patch, she then attempts to fix her hair. She huffs, "I feel so icky but the show must go on. Okay, Jason, start filming."

The small spotlight from the digital video camera shines starkly on Courtney's face.

"We're live," Jason announces.

Courtney does her best to muster a cutesy persona despite her queasy stomach. With a jittery voice she says, "Ahoy matey, this is Cortney the Buccaneer, broadcasting in real time from an actual rowboat off the shore of Charles Island! Just in time for Halloween. This is a restricted area! Off limits to the public. In a few moments, we'll have exclusive drone footage of the island's haunted beach. The fog out here on the water is very cool! Really spooky. Let's give a big shout-out to my peeps in Milford! What's all this drama about? Hello? Could it be the curse of Captain Kidd? At midnight, I will be interviewing an amazing psychic right here, onboard our boat. Mega fun, right?! She will be conjuring up the ghost of the famous pirate to get some answers! Personally, I hope he's sexy like Johnny Depp. Tweet me! Show some love for yours truly, Courtney The Buccaneer. First hundred fans will get free, Courtney The Buccaneer t-shirts!"

On cue, Jason hands the camera over to Courtney and begins to launch the drone. A high-pitched buzz is created by the whirling little propellers. The drone lifts skyward and zips off. Shrouded by the fog, it flies in the direction of Charles Island.

Moving her head about too much, Courtney is triggered to vomit a second time. She swallows back her barf.

A mere five seconds tick-by and the batteries on all of the electronics spontaneously go dead.

"I just lost connection with the drone," Jason says with concern.

"What?!" Courtney snaps.

"There is no signal," Jason replies. "Well, fix it!" orders Courtney. "I'm trying," Jason huffs.

"I-I don't feel good," rasps Ruth. "My lungs! It's-it's hard to breathe."

Courtney again gulps down her bile then cries, "You better not ruin this for me!"

Baffled, Jason says "The power sources are drained on the equipment."

Unexpectedly, the water then becomes oddly still. The rhythm of the lapping waves diminishes. The fog appears to stop shifting and freezes in place. There is splashing near the left side of the rowboat.

"Hey!" shouts Ed. "I think I just saw someone swim by!" "Stop fooling around!" Courtney whines.

Ed replies, "I'm not joking!"

There is tapping sounds on the underside of the craft. Courtney gasps, "Who's knocking?"

"Something just passed below us!" Exclaims Ed.

Faint hissing and moaning reverberates across the water. "Do you hear that?" Ed says.

"Are we being punked?!" Courtney asks with frightened anger.

The hissing in the mist starts to grow louder.

"It's –it's real!" Ruth stutters. "They, they- they-"

"Are you pulling my chain?" Ed snaps. He is starting to get genuinely creeped-out.

The intensity of the hissing is mounting. It echoes in the surrounding murk.

Ruth blurts, "They're-they're t-t-trying to-to channel me!" A rippling current starts to encircle the boat.

Ed panics and yells at Ruth, "What the fuck is going on?"

Ruth's eyes roll back in her head and she is stricken with a grand mal seizure. The hissing erupts into a shrill garble of wailing and hyena-like snarls. Convulsing, Ruth gnashes down hard. She then spits out the tip of her chewed-off tongue in a bloody froth. Courtney starts to uncontrollably tremble with terror then hurls the last of her stomach contents.

Ed hollers, "Fuck this! We're rowing back to shore!" He grabs both oars.

The banshee-like howling is now deafening.

"What about my drone?" Jason whimpers to himself while clamping his ears with his palms.

A whirlpool forms under the rowboat. The craft begins to spin.

Ed yells, "WHOA!!"

An unearthly centrifugal force causes the rowboat to splinter as if it was grinding in a wood chipper. Ruth goes ass-over-teakettle and instantly sinks. Courtney and Jason swirl about for a second. Thrashing about with his arms and legs, Ed desperately attempts to swim out of the whirlpool but is also taken down into the aquatic black hole. The surface of the water returns to an abnormally placid state while at the very bottom, a gyrating force accelerates into a churning blur. It is not drowning but rather a lethal whiplash effect that kills all four. Their clothes are ripped off their bodies in the rotational blender. Soon their naked corpses are spun together into a large meaty ball of flesh and fractured bones. Slurry of silt, debris and pulverized bluefish is added to the mix.

At the strike of midnight, the 697 pounds of compacted human tissue and other organic matter, rockets from the sea floor and explodes from the surface of Long Island Sound. In a rising column of salt water, the gruesome mass is propelled 40 thousand feet into the atmosphere.

Monday Oct.
29th 00:01 Hours

On night patrol, Special Agent Ortiz is smoking a cigarette while standing on the east shore of Charles Island. He turns to his partner, Miller and asks, "Did you hear something out there on the water?"

"Nah," says Miller. "Everything is so quiet tonight except for these frigging mosquitos." Miller then slaps his sweaty neck. "This fog is intense."

"Can't see shit," says Ortiz.

Behind their backs and up on the embankment, Phillip is out of his hole again. Hidden in the darkness, he lurks by the crumbling brick archway of the old Aquinas chapel. Bestowed with new abilities, Phillip can see perfectly clear through the mist. From his vantage point, he witnessed from afar what happened to the four people on the rowboat. He was also allowed to hear every hellish sound associated with their demise. Phillip smirks, then whispers, "What goes up, must come down."

Monday Oct.
29th 00:06 Hours

Six members of the Ecumenical Christian chorus group are returning home late to Milford Connecticut from a world peace rally held in Central Park. Their beige Dodge Caravan is on I-95. A mile away from the exit ramp, a half ton hunk of ice, debris, and human remains comes barreling down from the foggy night sky. The roof of the mini-van instantly collapses as the giant frozen object makes a direct hit. The occupant's skulls and and spinal columns are compacted down into their pelvises. All four tires on the vehicle explode. Windshield glass pulverizes. Bumpers and door panels go flying. The main frame of the Dodge Caravan is flattened and pressed down into the cratering asphalt. Chain reaction collisions occur on the interstate. A semi plows on top of a Prius. Other rigs jack knife.

The members of the Ecumenical Christian chorus group
would never know what the hell hit them.

Monday Oct. 29th

11:05 Hours

FBI special investigator William Dover had flown in from Quantico. He sits in the backseat of a black Ford Explorer. They are parked at the entrance of Silver Sands. A state trooper is the driver. The two other passengers are local field agents. Dover was informed that a commercial flight coming from Bradley picked up an unidentified object when crossing Long Island Sound. The pilots thought it was a bogey. Preliminary identifications were made on the victims riding in the van on I-95. Other human remains have been discovered at the scene. The forensic team is perplexed and trying to determine how many fatalities were actually involved. Bits of marine life were also detected in the chunks of frozen sea water.

A light drizzle patters and beads on the windshield of the SUV. Dover zips up his dark blue parker and says softly, "I want to start here first. I'm going to take a walk around the island. You three can remain in the vehicle."

Dover exits the Ford Explorer. He steps out onto the empty stretch of beach. Silver Sands Park is now off limits to the public. It is a grey day but the ambience is still muggy. There are no seagulls. An abnormal stillness reigns except for the lapping of the surf. It is low-tide and the sandbar is exposed. Off to the left, the small summer rental commandeered by the authorities continues to be utilized. Dover chooses to keep walking toward the tombolo. He crosses the barriers of orange cones and yellow-police tape. Making it on to the sandbar, there is the ominous sense that the dark water aligning both sides of the path could suddenly surge up and drown him. The stench of rotting fish is heavy.

Without warning, there comes the thumping of rotary blades. A Coast Guard helicopter passes overhead on lookout for Porto, the missing diver. Early in the morning, a two-man rescue sub was employed but still came up with nothing.

A few droplets of light rain hits Dover's cheek. He welcomes the stimuli. The feeling of wetness grounds him for a moment. For the last five nights, he has been wide wake. The sleep deprivation causes him to be spacey and preoccupied. Dover is tall and gaunt with a greying crew cut. The recent insomnia makes the man appear even more aged. Being assigned to help with the investigation seemed oddly predetermined. Dover had never once been to Milford but he was often plagued by childhood nightmares of being lost in woods on a little island in the middle of nowhere.

"Deja vu." Dover utters to himself as he finishes the half- mile trek on the sandbar and makes it onto the island.

A ring of rocky beach encircles the small, straggly forest. Dover trudges up the embankment of seashells and pebbles. He pauses for a moment on top of the plateau and stares into the woods. All of the heron nests in the leafless trees are empty. Creaking and snapping disrupts the unnerving stillness. It is wind-polluted with the stink of carrion that rustles through the hanging dead branches. Epizootic Hemorrhagic Disease has killed a herd of whitetails on the island. The dear carcasses are decomposing in the underbrush and writing with maggots and fiddler crabs.

Dover had planned to stay on the periphery of the island but at this present moment, he finds himself hypnotized and propelled into its interior. Tangled brambles of fallen tree limbs impede every step. Overhead, clouds grow dense and oppressive. The natural light of day is being engulfed with a dusk-like gloom.

"It's getting dark," Dover says aloud. His sleeve to his rain parker gets hung up on prickers. He pulls his arm away and rips the GORE-TEX material. An abrupt sense of panic is triggered and Dover races forward. He plows deeper into the forest, almost twisting his ankle. Surging adrenaline mutes the pain from all the scratches and pokes from the thicket.

Suddenly, Dover stops as he hears a human voice.

The voice shouts, "Officer down! Officer down! Officer needs assistance!"

Dover then sees a man come staggering out of the brush. The stranger also appears lost and confused. Dover observes that the man is holding the right side of his head. The man's sports jacket is torn from the branches and soaked with red blotches. The seat of his beige trousers is stained brown.

"What happened?" Dover asks.

"Officer down! Officer down! Officer needs assistance now!" the man cries.

"Who-who are you?" Dover stammers.

Whimpering, the man says, "I'm detective Helminski. Look at what that bitch made me do." The man then lowers his hand from the side of his head, revealing the bullet hole in his temple. It is a jagged star-shaped contact wound with sooty stippling. In the next second, streams of blood come pouring out of Helminski's nostrils.

Dover attempts to scream as he is flooded with a nightmarish sense of vertigo. He falls backward. Before Dover hits the ground, he losses consciousness and is enveloped in blackness.

Monday Oct. 29th

12:21 Hours

"Officer needs assistance! Officer needs assistance!" shouts special agent Ortiz as he calls into his mic.

Dover's eyelids flicker as he regains consciousness. He is lying flat on his back on the outer shore of the island. There is a patchwork of scratches on his face and hands. His rain jacket is ripped and torn. Attempting to focus, Dover looks up at the two young men in their black tactical fatigues.

"Sir, we called for a medevac," says special agent Miller. "We are here to help you."

"Where am I?" Dover gasps. "How did I get here?"

"We observed you staggering out of the woods. You came onto the beach and just collapsed here a moment ago."

"I need to get up," Dover groans.

"Please sir, stay put until medevac arrives." "Hel-Hel-Helminski," Dover stutters.

Ortiz and Miller shoot each other inquisitive glances.

"Must leave," Dover says as he struggles to a seated position on the ground. His head is swooning. His left ankle is throbbing with pain.

In the next moment, there comes the sound of muffled buzzing. It then sputters and stalls.

The buzzing starts up again. "What is that?" barks Miller.

"I don't know," responds Ortiz. "It seems to be coming from over there." Ortiz points to the old stone archway up on the nearby embankment.

"Want me to check it out?" asks Miller. "Yeah, I'll stay with him," nods Ortiz.

With his Colt M4 slung on his back, Special Agent Miller quickly trots toward the incline leading up to the ruins. He bounds up the slope of wet sand and shells. Reaching the top of the embankment, he pauses. The buzzing grows louder. Miller notices that the earth in front of the stone archway is disturbed. There is a hole in the ground.

"What the heck?" Miller says to himself.

The buzzing sound is coming from inside the hole. Dropping to his knees, Miller leans forward and peers into the burrow. Against all protocol and wisdom, the young agent finds himself blindly reaching into the dark hole.

Why the hell am I doing this? he says to himself.

On cue, the buzzing stops. With a searching hand, Miller feels around and touches moist plastic. He pulls the object out of the burrow.

Ortiz calls out from below on the shore, "What is it?" Dover continues to sit and shiver.

Miller stands up, wiping the wet sand off the object. He yells back to Ortiz, "It's a drone!"

Monday Oct. 29th
14:03 Hours

Principal Shaffer is in his office being besieged with phone calls from hysterical parents and jittery faculty. The Milford public schools continue to be closed until further notice. Taking a deep breath, Shaffer pauses and prays for guidance.

Dear Jesus, please show me the way!

The next second, an internal alarm comes blaring through the PA system. A cry for assistance sounds on the principal's walkie-talkie Instantly, Shaffer finds himself running down the hall toward the school cafeteria. The security guard is already there at the doorway to the lunchroom.

"My god!" gasps Shaffer as he halts at the entrance. "How did he get in here?"

"I don't know!" shouts the trembling security guard. "The police are on their way!"

It is an odd scene with a large empty cafeteria and a single student sitting alone at a lunch table. The boy is voraciously gorging himself. Numerous pints of milk and chocolate brownies have been pilfered from the school kitchen. There is also a brown paper bag near the pile of snacks. Animalistic sounds of famished feeding echoes in the vastness of the room.

Shaffer stutters, "Ph-Ph-Phillip is that you?"

The Zika-infected mosquito bite has swollen into a black and blue malignant mass on his forehead. Almost every inch of the boy's pasty white skin is marred with abrasions and cuts. His black tee shirt and black jeans are encrusted with dried blood and wet sand. He stinks of death, urine, and the sea. Streams of milk pour down his chin as he gulps down another container. His small teeth are coated with thick yellow tarter and now bits of chocolate brownie.

Shaffer asks with a shaky voice, "Where have you been, Phillip?"

Phillip stops eating for a moment and says with a crazed smile, "Hey Principal Shaffer, what's the final verdict on dairy? Skim? 2 percent? Lactose-free? I'm confused. Ah, fuck it! I'll drink'em all." The boy guzzles a fifth half pint and burps loudly.   He then asks "By the way, where is everybody? Why the mass hooky?"

With sweat stains growing under his armpits, Shaffer says, "We were really concerned about you?"

Chewing a brownie with an open mouth and speaking at the same time, Phillip says "Charles Island is my new celebrity crib. I should have stayed in my hole, but I was so fucking hungry. Ever try to catch a seagull and eat it raw? Those birds are mean bitches. The thing pecked the shit out of my arm and got away."

"Your mother has been really worried," Shaffer states in metered tone while trying to control his fear.

A flash of rage shines in Phillip's wild blue eyes. Dropping his smile, he says in a voice much older than his own, "In the fog, I walked back on the sandbar. I made it home before dawn.   Crept into that dump-of-a-house like a ninja. Her worrying didn't stop her from drinking. As usual, I found her passed-out in her recliner.

Finally decided to do my own special intervention. Afterward, I went to the fridge, and wouldn't you know it! Not one scrap of food. Just some bottles of chilled Bukoff. That's why I came here for a late lunch."

Sounds of approaching sirens are heard in the distance. The security guard is counting the seconds. With chills going up his spine, Shaffer asks, "Is-is your mom, okay?"

Phillip glares back, appearing at any second that he will go berserk and charge at the two middle-aged men. The boy's malicious smiles returns.

"Let me show you something." Phillip says in an abrupt, jolly manner. His voice is now high-pitched and almost feminine. He reaches out for the brown paper bag sitting on the lunch table.

"I don't like this!" says the security guard, "What's he got in that bag?"

Shaffer knows he should run but freezes in his tracks.

"Calm down," laughs Phillip. "I don't have a gun." Phillip lifts up the brown paper bag. Dark blood starts to come through on the bottom.

"Woops, I guess the zip-lock failed." Phillip feigns embarrassment and giggles. "We have leakage!" He then reaches into the bag and pulls out a slippery red organ. The men are aghast as they witness the horror.

"This is my dessert I have been saving for last. It's my mother's cancerous uterus. I cut it out of her corpse this morning." With gusto, Phillip bites down hard on the smooth muscle tissue. He rips off a piece of uterus with his teeth and swallows it. Blood drips down from his chin mixing with milk. He leers at the trembling men and proclaims in a guttural snarl, "THIS IS HOW MUCH I FUCKIN' HATE WHERE I CAME FROM!"

Wednesday Oct. 31th

11:55 Hours

It is again unnaturally warm weather for autumn. Over a thousand residents of Milford, plus the media have shown up for a town vigil on Gulf Beach. Across the bay, Silver Sands park continues to remain closed. Not far from shore, Charles Island is in plain view. It is a foreboding dark place in contrast to the bright blue sky and calm waters of the day. A platform and podium has been erected near the Gulf Beach wharf. Various church groups and religious organizations are in attendance to offer prayers and comfort to the community. There is also a heavy police presence.

The mayor of Milford is a short portly man. He is wearing an I Luv Courtney the Buccaneer tee shirt in remembrance, as are some others in the crowd. The tee shirt is too small and is stretched tightly across his pot belly. Walking up to the podium, the mayor adjusts the microphone, clears his throat and begins to speak with dramatic resonance, "In 1777, on this very spot, a British ship set ashore 46 patriots stricken with smallpox. They were prisoners of our country's revolutionary war. Captain Stowe and other residences of this fine town cared for those sick men. They all died of the disease. So did Captain Stowe. What did not die, was the memory of their sacrifice and courage!"

The mayor turns and point's outward.

"In 1933 three parishioners built a shrine on Charles' Island.

When returning to shore on Easter Sunday their boat capsized. All drowned. What did not die, was the memory of their devotion! I talk about the past, only to help us with today. At the present moment our beautiful town has been overwhelmed with tragedy upon tragedy. There are many unanswered questions. People are still missing. There has been so many unexplained deaths. I know you are scared. But we have the courageous folks here, from local law enforcement, the FBI and Homeland Security, to make things right! Let's show them our deep appreciation and give them a round of applause!" The mayor starts clapping.

Cheers and boos erupt from the crowd.

Grieving relatives yell out, "We want answers! We deserve answers!"

The major raises his hand and replies, "Yes! I want a resolution just like you. In this time of uncertainty, please care for one another. The waiting is hard. Many hurricanes have damaged our beloved Milford, but we always rebuild. I am certain all of us can weather this storm too!"

The clamor of voices of agreement, mixed with shouts of anger, are growing louder. He had prepared a much longer speech but the mayor feels a building tension in the crowd. He quickly turns his attention to the church groups in attendance. Tapping the mic, the mayor says, "At this moment, please bow your heads and take time to listen to some hymns that inspire strength."

In tribute to the ecumenical chorus members killed on I-95, the choirs had collaborated on a piece of music for the event. On cue from the mayor, they start singing.

"Rise up! Rise-up! Rise-up! Those who are in fear, rise-up!
Rise-up…"

Some in the crowd balk while others attempt to sing along.
Many weep. The sounds carry out across the bay. It is a haunting
melancholy murmur.

"Rise-up. Rise-up! Those who are in pain, rise-up! Rise-up…"

The mayor exhales to calm his anxiety.

"Rise-up.

Rise-up.

Rise-up those who are lost, rise-up!

Rise-up…"

At first, no one on the beach spots the small black head
bobbing up from the surface of the water. It is far in the distance,
out near Charles Island. As the singing continues, the figure moves
closer. It is low tide. Soon the head and shoulders are exposed.
Then the upper torso. A figure in a wetsuit is approaching the shore
of Gulf Beach.

As the figure is noticed, many think it is just a swimmer. None
suspect that it is Porto. The rescue diver is not close enough yet for
them to see his state of decomposition. Porto's body has been
putrefying in saltwater for over a week. A grey-greenish, nibbled,
tongue protrudes from his lipless mouth. His nose, left eye, and most
of the flesh of his face has been eaten away by porgies and striped
sea robins. Goggles are missing but he continues to wear the
neoprene diver's hood. The remaining eyeball bulges from its
socket and is coated with a white slime. Trillions of bacteria cause a
bloating effect with rotting entrails expanding with fetid gas.

Appearing as if the diver is pregnant, the black wet suit bulges at the abdomen. The air tank and respirator are long gone, but Porto continues to wear a single right flipper. In a clumsy stagger, he walks in the gentle surf.

Onshore, Porto's family is present. His five-year-old daughter looks out and with tears streaming down her cheeks, suddenly shrieks, "DADDY!" Porto's wife gasps, thinking that it is a cruel Halloween prank.

Nearby, spectators start shouting. A few rush forward, assuming it is a wounded swimmer in need of medical care. The mayor sees a photo opportunity and quickly waddles down the podium and heads toward the figure in the surf. Milford police officers start running across the beach, alerted by the commotion.

Still attached to Porto's diving belt is a SOG Bowie. The blade is over 7 inches long and is partially serrated. As people approach, Porto quickly draws the knife in a sweeping arch. A teenage boy, the first within proximity, is cut on the bicep. A white girl with dreads gets slashed across the chest. Confused and screaming, some start to run away from the knife-wielding zombie, while others keep coming.

"We need assistance here! We need assistance here!" shouts the mayor.

An unnatural animating energy propels Porto to lunge onto the beach. The zombie-diver goes straight after the pudgy little man wearing the I Luv Courtney The Buccaneer tee shirt. The mayor turns and attempts to flee. Porto jabs the SOG Bowie into the top of the mayor's head. With a loud crunch, the blade enters at the center of the bald spot and pierces deep into the brain. The curved tip of the knife comes poking out from under the mayor's double chin.

Pounding with adrenaline, the first cop to make it through the crowd freezes in disbelief as he sees the thing yank the Bowie free from the mayor's skull with a spray of red droplets.

A second officer comes on the scene, drawing his Sig Sauer and shouting, "Drop the goddam knife!"

The mayor's body is now on the ground, twitching. Porto raises up the knife and takes a step forward. With jittering hands, the second officer starts blasting away with his service pistol. Ejected brass shell-casings fly into the air. Bullets easily pass through the decaying flesh of the zombie-diver. A stray round grazes a spectator's shin. A couple of .40 caliber hollow points hit Porto in the lower torso. The bulging neoprene wet suit splits open at the belly. A foul-smelling gaseous eruption is accompanied by the sound of fifty deflating and sputtering balloons. Coils of brownish-ochre, rotting intestines come spilling out on to the sand. The stench causes all those in the immediate vicinity to instantly gag and vomit. Porto collapses into a motionless heap. It is all caught on Instagram.

Wednesday Oct. 31th

18:01 Hours

Dover is sitting across a table from Phillip in an interview room at the Connecticut River Hills Psychiatric Institute. In the hallway are two other FBI agents and a team of hospital security guards.

"I'll stop talking if anyone else comes in here," warns Phillip.

"We'll respect that," replies Dover in a consolatory tone.

"Let's chat. Just you and I."

Phillip loudly exhales and says, "I wanted to see you the day I got here but they had me comatose on Haldol and Thorazine. Being in four-point restraints for days sucks. My wrists fucking hurt."

There is a sterile white bandage on the teenager's forehead. An exorbitant volume of puss had been drained from the monstrous Zika infected abscess. Multiple cuts and peck marks have scabbed over on Phillip's chubby arms. His light blue Johnny coat is stained with grape juice and covered with cookie crumbs.

Dover nods. His mock sympathy is transparent.

Phillip glares at the FBI agent with greater intensity and says, "Be careful, I can read your mind. You believe that I'm just a common psychopath. Is that right, William?"

Raising an eyebrow, Dover stares back.

Phillip smirks. "Have you finally gotten some sleep? You still seem beat. Worn out. Gosh, look at those dark circles under your eyes. Those scratches healing up? Ankle better? When you were lost in the woods, you were such a space cadet. Fucking hilarious. Your colleagues are concerned that you are on the verge of having a nervous breakdown. It is not just me; they're monitoring your mental stability too. At any moment, they'll pull you off this case if you start acting wacky again. Make sure you don't put a bullet through your head or set yourself on fire, okay, William?"

Stiffening in his chair, Dover says coldly, "So, you were watching me that day on Charles Island?"

"No." Phillip laughs. "I left in the morning before you came across on the sandbar."

"Interesting," Dover says, feeling his stomach tightening.

Phillip's smirk turns into a vicious grin. "You know what else is interesting? Your cousin is in the CIA. Right now, he's on assignment near the Dead Sea in the middle east. Your family must be so proud of you two boys. One in the FBI. The other a covert spook. True American heroes."

This time Dover cannot maintain his cool demeanor. Alarm flashes in his eyes. He blurts out, "Where did you get this information?!"

Rocking back in his chair, the teenager claps his hands and hoots as if he just won a game of Monopoly. Phillip then leans forward and becomes immediately stern. "I know you want answers, William. You are so frightened inside. Remember those recurrent nightmares you had as a child? Being lost in the woods on that little island in the middle of nowhere. It was all precognition."

Dover stutters, "Who-who, the fuck are you?"

Sounding instantly cheerful, the kid answers, "I am Phillip Sanford, descendent of Mary Sanford. She was hung as a witch in1662 in Hartford. Her husband escaped here to Milford. You can see his tombstone in the town graveyard. Do you know that Milford has the oldest active cemetery in America! Awesome, right?"

Chills run up Dover's spine.

"But wait!" Phillip exclaims. "I can tell your getting the wrong idea. What is happening is not some trite ancient curse. Theories about witches and pirates irk the fuck out of me. It's all paranormal bullshit! So lame! I know Homeland Security boys are going for the scientific angle. They hypothesize that maybe some biological or chemical nerve agent is causing people to go ape shit in this town. No! Wrong again! The truth is far more, like…Wow!"

Swallowing hard, Dover demands, "Tell me what is really happening!"

Gloating, Phillip taps the table and says in a patronizing voice, "Uhh, I'm sorry but when a farmer slaughters a cow, a pig, or a chicken, does he explain the reason to the animal? Of course not; that would be silly. The livestock are too dumb to understand. Right now, the population of the world is reaching 8 billion people. When Charles Island blooms, there will be trillions of "the others" marching across that sandbar. Let's just say, mankind is fucked, and leave it at that."

"You're delusional!" Dover replies.

"Wishful thinking!" Phillip barks back. He then asks coyly, "By the way, what did you see in the video footage from the drone? You know, the drone that was found in my hole in the ground."

During the past week, Dover and his investigation team had been analyzing the murky footage. It is less than thirty seconds in duration. There is a quick snippet of a naked female figure. Her pale whiteness is in contrast to the darkness of the scene. She is leaning over and writing something in the sand.

"Who is the girl in the drone footage?" asks Dover. "Crystal," replies Phillip. "But don't worry about her. You have to watch out for The Hammer."

"What?" Dover replies. He starts to visibly tremble.

With his seething, crazy blue eyes, Phillips snarls at the FBI agent and hisses, "Enough said. Interview is now over. Run for your life, William. Happy Halloween."

Wednesday Oct. 31th

19:13 Hours

The police SUV with red lights flashing is racing back to Milford. A state trooper is driving. Dover sits in the back of the vehicle with two other field agents. Attempting to suppress his shaking left leg, Dover appears blood-drained and teetering on the brink of insanity.

One of the agents says with a jittery voice, "We just got report that a two man LR5 was destroyed. It was exploring an egress under the surface of Charles's Island. They say the sub got crushed like a tin can."

"The fucking place needs to be officially quarantined!" shouts the other agent.

Dover mutters, "Where do we run?"

Wednesday Oct. 31th

19:14 Hours

Air force pilot Roy Connor has turned off communications in his cockpit. He had recently been scrambled from OTIS after NORAD ordered an air patrol of the Connecticut coast. The F-16 rips through the night sky at Mach 2. With a sonic boom that shatters windows in apartment buildings, the jet exits Massachusetts and passes over the city of Hartford.

Connor says aloud, "Mary Sanford? Who just whispered that name in my head?"

Having flown over three hundred sorties in Iraq and Afghanistan, Connor has racked up an impressive amount of kills. His crew gave him the moniker, The Hammer. He has been crafty about burying his PTSD but at this very moment, an entity has infiltrated his mental defenses. With a hissing voice, it taunts and triggers the pilot. The man's suicidal proclivity is a perfect recipe for an explosion of agony and rage. With his fragile will hijacked, Connor veers the plane south toward the Milford shoreline. The entity giggles and tells the Hammer about the first target.

Wednesday Oct. 31th

19:20 Hours

At Connecticut River Hill Psychiatric Institute, a nurse screams in terror while a mental health tech watches in awe. Philip Sanford is alone in his seclusion room, levitating near the ceiling. The boy's Johnnie coat is crumbled on the bed. With arms out stretched, Philip is naked. His small, uncircumcised albino penis is erect. Infected bug bites and crisscross scratches mar his flabby body. Giggling like a toddler, his eyes roll back in his head and he starts making jetfighter sounds as he floats around the room.

Wednesday Oct. 31th

19:40 Hours

Sweat beads roll down Dover's temple as he continues to ride along in the back of the SUV. He is waiting like a prisoner on death row. Dangerously, his blood pressure is peaking. The other three men have stopped talking. They too have a foreboding sense of doom as they get closer to Milford.

Dover breaks the silence and says, "When will the other shoe drop?"

The Connecticut Department of Transportation has repaired the crater in the stretch of highway near the Milford exit ramp. From ten miles away in the night sky, there comes a quick horizontal streak of light. Connor has fired a laser-guided, air-to-ground missile. The Maverick E2 rocket hits the police SUV at the exact spot where the Dodge Caravan got squashed. All four men in the Ford Explorer do not have time to suffer. With a blinding yellow flash, the searing heat and tremendous air pressure sucks the oxygen from their exploding lungs. They instantly die in the obliterating explosion. Liquefying plastic and melting steel mixes with carbonizing flesh. The rear half of the trans-axial flies into the air.

"The Hammer pounds another nail!" Connor cheers aloud in the cockpit of his plane.

The pilot starts to maneuver the F-16 toward downtown Milford. Connor plans to strafe the old churches with the jetfighter's

20 millimeter Vulcan Gatling cannon. There are now multiple voices in his head, egging him on in a shrill chorus. They sing, KILL MORE! KEEP KILLING! KILL THEM ALL! KILL!"

Wednesday Oct. 31th

19:49 Hours

Homeland Security Agent, Ortiz is panicky. His partner, Miller has not returned yet from taking a shit in the forest and he just got word that all patrols are to cease. New quarantine plans are to be implemented. Ortiz is also unnerved by the sounds of distant explosions and sirens.

"What the fuck is blowing up?" Ortiz says with alarm in his voice.

It is low tide and the sandbar is exposed. The water appears placid with a metallic hue from the glow of the moon. It would be easy to walk back to Silver Sands Beach but another order was sent out warning that no personnel is to cross the tombolo on foot. The last contact from the command center, said that a police boat would come out to retrieve Ortiz and Miller from Charles Island.

Standing on the embankment, Ortiz turns, peers into the dense black woods and shouts, "Miller, goddamn it! What's taking so long? Answer me?"

There are no signs of his partner. The forest is a black walk of daunting stillness. Not even a dead branch creaks. Ortiz looks back toward the mainland. The warmth of civilization seams far away from the island. He then notices that there is not one Coast Guard vessel on patrol.

Ortiz says to himself, "Where did everyone go? Why am I

alone out here?"

Pressing the button on his field mic, communications are dead. Instinctively, he brings up his Colt M4 but there is no one to point the weapon at. The rifle suddenly feels puny and ineffective in his hands.

In frightened desperation Ortiz yells again, "Miller where the fuck are you?"

The dark woods beckon.

Don't go in there! Ortiz pleads with himself.

In the next second, Ortiz finds himself unslinging his weapon, dropping it on the ground and stepping forward into the forest. Like the others, his will is no longer is own.

Wednesday Oct. 31th

23:01 Hours

The sound of harsh static coming from the field mic, breaks the unnatural silence of the night. Ortiz slowly comes out of his fugue state. He finds himself on all fours staring into the dark hole at the foot of the old chapel ruins. It is the same hole that Phillip had hid in and where the drone was found. Ortiz's left cornea is scratched after being poked by a branch. There are other cuts and scrapes on his body from walking through the dark forest in a dissociative trance.

"Christ! How did I get here?" the agent shouts in terror as he jumps up.

Down on the outer shore of the island, there is a tall, thin woman. She is naked. Bending over, she is writing something in the wet sand with her finger. Her alabaster skin glistens in the shimmering moonlight.

"Who are you?" shouts Ortiz.

Pretending to be startled, she quickly rises and scampers into the surf. With a couple of splashes and kicks from her long legs, the woman disappears under the water. Ortiz then notices a large fleshy mound on the beach. Stumbling on the slope of shale and shells, the agent hurries down from the chapel ruins onto the shore.

Scrawled in the wet sand is the message, GO POUND SAND UP YOUR ASS. It is signed, Crystal.

Ortiz then runs to the nearby large mass and instantly halts.

The grotesque horror is sensory overload. Miller is still wearing his tactical boots but his gear is missing. Having been stuffed to over five-hundred-pounds, his uniform had stretched and tore off in tatters. Thousands upon thousands of busted capillaries are a spidery network on his mega taunt dermis. Miller's eyes bulge out of their sockets in shock. Fine grains of sand pour from his ears and nostrils. Miller's cheeks are stuffed with clam shells. "What the hell happened to you!" Ortiz screams. In the next second, a spout of sand and pebbles shoots up from the ground and hits Ortiz between the legs. The sodomizing force rips a hole in the seat of his black tactical pants. A stream of granules enters his anus. Instantly, Ortiz's rectum becomes full of sand. His perineum is exfoliated raw as more sand packs into his colon. In the passing of another moment, all 27 feet of intestines are humongous stuffed sausages of sand. There are sharp popping sounds as his pelvic fractures. Ortiz's tummy is flooded next. Like a bursting oil rig, blood, feces, gastric juices mixes with the sand and blows out of his mouth. The violating surge is greater this time, causing both of Ortiz's eye balls to explode from their sockets.

The old chapel ruins are glowing red.

Wednesday Oct. 31th

23:49 Hours

Kevin, a young reporter with a local cable news channel, has not heeded the order to vacate the area. Bob, his cameraman, is also amped to the max with exhilaration. Both believe this could be their big moment to be witnesses to history. They are near the road at the entrance to Silver Sand's State Park. National Guard trucks full of edgy troops zoom by. Nervously, Kevin tries to pat down his almost perfect hair. He is wearing a rain jacket as if he were out in the field reporting on an approaching storm. The spot light is stark and makes his complexion appear anemic.

"We are here reportedly on events as they unfold," announces Kevin as he stares into the camera with wide eyes, "Tonight, there is chaos and terror in the town of Milford. This is not a Halloween hoax! Reportedly, all the churches are ablaze and nearly destroyed; a jet fighter appeared to deliberately fly into the local green; residents continue to flee; highways are parking lots clogged with traffic.

"We are unsure of who is responsible for, what is believed to be, a 'terrorist' act! People escaping from the shore describe seeing thousands of "them", coming across from Charles Island. There are police barricades in front of us at the entrance to the beach, but we plan to sneak in and try to discover what they mean by "them"!

A man in a tattered sports jacket and soiled beige pants comes stumbling into view. He appeared to just materialize. The man is holding the right side of his misshapen head. At first, Kevin thinks the frumpy guy is intoxicated but then he observes all the crusted dried blood.

The reporter addresses the man with excitement, "Sir, it is clearly evident that you are injured! What happened? Where are you coming from?"

Slurring, the man answers, "I j-j-just came from Charles Island."

"Charles Island!?" exclaims Kevin.

"Yeah, I walked across the sandbar with the others. Officer down! Officer down! Officer needs assistance!"

"Sir, what's your name? Can you tell us what you saw?" "My name is Detective Helminski! I-I-I got to run,

Crystal is coming!"

Quickly, Helminski staggers out of view from the camera. In the distance, a crowd of moving shadows pour from the entrance to the park. There are growing sounds of hissing and snarling. Bob, the cameraman sees her first but keeps rolling. Behind the reporter, the tall naked form of a woman rapidly approaches with silent, stalking steps. Her hair is wet and slicked back. Moonlight makes her moist skin appear to have a blue, white glow but cast her hallow eye sockets in darkness. Her cheeks are full of shards of sea shells. Kevin turns just as she spits the shards in a forceful stream. The fragments of seashells tear into the reporter's upper chest and face like shrapnel from a hand grenade. A nasty jagged bit of razor-like clam shell splits his left carotid artery. Gagging and whimpering, Kevin holds his neck as blood spurts from between his fingers. He falls on the ground.

Next, Bob the cameraman, is slaughtered. Then... all of mankind.

Dudleytown

Connecticut Extreme Horror

A. Sanford

Smithfield, England 1553

The wine was the finest he had ever drunk but it gave him no joy. It is an hour before dawn. Two mice boldly gnaw away at the brat ruben laying in the middle of the straw pile that is his bed. Unlike the vermin, Edward Sanford has no appetite. His nausea is great. A mixture of Malmsey, gastric juices and cheddar cheese had been vomited on the stone floor. Sour is the stench that pollutes the prison cell. Bug bites pock Edward's anemic skin. His emaciated arms and torso are bare to the assault. Since his miserable birth, Edward has known the nips of fleas but the insects in this dank chamber appear more ferocious. He slaps and scratches his flank.

"How ye devour me so! Damn, these little nasties!"

The henchman had left proper leggings, trousers, and a fine shirt of linen but Edward dare not put them on.

"Rogues want me to wear such finery as part of a disguise. But those garments are thy death costume!" Edward then cries aloud, "'Tis a very wicked dream in which I cannot awake!"

Edward is a thief that turned into a murderer after pushing a dotard into the Thames. The two had been fighting over a tuppence. Initially, Edward had accepted his fate to be hung as a common criminal but of recent, he has been given a more hellish demise. Edward never cared for the affairs of the royals. The acrimony between the Catholics and Protestants was not his passion. A deep hatred for Christianity was imbued into Edward at a very young age. His toothless Auntie often spoke of the wondrous sunrise during Alban Hefin. She prayed to an entity that dwelled among the hedges. The folks in the shire did not take kindly to her pagan beliefs so they beat her with broom handles in hopes of ridding her of the devil. Her frail constitution was unable to survive such attention.

Edward whimpers, "Now I too have been given a similar fate but with grander agony. What a strange change of fortune, that I, a son of a whore, be a surrogate for another of regal blood!"

As of recent, members of the family of Dudley have been convicted of subversion. A few had already lost their heads at Tower Hill. Those loyal to the Dudleys had concocted a plan to save one of the condemned. Henchman rummaged the local jails, searching for a subject of similar height and stature. Edward was chosen. They beat his face and marred it with a good rubbing of stinging nettles to make it swell. In the darkness of night, the young royal Dudley absconded away from his prison cell along with the henchmen. Edward was left in his place to endure the punishment for high treason.

"A promise was made that the executioner will be paid well to hang me in a fashion that there would be no lasting suffering. Doe'st trust scoundrels? Is treachery so easily forgiven because they tossed me a few scraps of luxury, a flask of Malmsey and a mouthful of fancy morsels?"

Wincing, Edward touches his bruised cheeks and split lip with his trembling fingertips.

"I know not how I look? There was no apology for the rough ways in which they treated thy flesh. They said only that thy features must be unrecognizable for the deception to be successful. Surely, my nose feels asunder."

With a shaky hand, Edward reaches down to cup his bollocks.

"Hath I dread the prospect of being drawn and quartered! I have seen rebels hast such ends. But I refuse to grovel to Jesus for mercy. His own omnipotent father let him linger on that cross for a good bit of time. But who do I turn to in thy darkest hour to calm thy terror?"

The mice continue to eat the roasted turnips while the fleas continued with their parasitic feasting. Edward doubles overs with cramps. His bowels are blocked and hurting as if constipated with hot coals.

"Moments linger! I fear dawn, yet I wish this maddening foreboding cease! Shall I weaken thy resolve and pray to Christ?"

Abruptly, the rodents are stricken with a sense of menace.

They scammer away from their bounty and dart into crevasses. Even the fleas jump off their host and vanish. In the darkened corner of the prison cell there comes a presence.

It hisses in an ancient language older than the Druids.

Edward stares into the mirk. Quivering, he gasps, "Doth hast madness in thy final hours? Is there a phantom in yon shadows that speaks? Are thou truly real?"

Far in the distance, a cock crows, signaling the start of day.

The bells of St. Bartholomew start to clang and echo.

***

It is a crisp morning with a bit of blue peeking through the oppressive clouds. Strapped on his back to a wooden sled, Edward is wide-eyed with panic. One may assume that the condemned wretch is desperately looking up to heaven, begging for deliverance but Edward's true and immediate concern is trying not to choke to death on his own blood. Earlier, the prison guards had entered his cell with long handled pincers and a pair of shears. They had been bribed to snip off the tip of the criminal's tongue. The crude surgery is insurance to prevent Edward from speaking out at the last moment and revealing the Dudley's deception. For good measure, the guards also trounced his face a bit more to make it a swollen bloody mask. Before Edward was dragged from his chamber and bound to the sled, he was forced to don the proper leggings, trousers and shirt of fine linen.

A soldier steps forward and whips the rump of the old white

horse. The animal pauses for a moment as it raises its tail. With another strike from its master, the beast of burden starts to draw the sled. Cackling and shouts of excitement erupt from the awaiting masses. A gauntlet of rabble have already aligned the muddy lane leading from the prison toward the butcher's market.

Ironically, Edward had been a spectator of numerous public executions at Smithfield. It was a fertile opportunity to pickpocket the distracted. At the present moment, fools that he had robbed and prostitutes that he had fucked are in the crowd, jeering, not knowing his identity.

The pelting begins and it is relentless. Stones, pig slop, dung balls and others sorts of repugnant objects rain down on Edward as he is towed along behind the tired nag. Brown water splashes about as the sled is dragged through mucky puddles. A cruel, cross-eyed boy barges out onto the path holding a wooden bucket. The pail is full of urine collected from three drunkards in attendance. The lad douses Edward with a shower of piss. Howls of delight burst from the mob. Someone takes a dead rat by the tail and flings it. The rodent, stiff with rigor mortis, beans off Edward's brow.

By the time Edward is drawn to the center of the butcher's market, he is soaked and splattered with refuse. His tresses of unwashed hair are tangled with debris. The proper leggings, trousers, and fine shirt of linen are the color of burnt umber and garbage. Dudley's henchman lurking in the crowd experience a bit of relief as they observe that Sanford's face is truly unrecognizable.

Besides being horribly battered, it is now concealed with filth. Incongruent with the happenings of the morning, more bright sunlight shines down from above and warms the gathered audience. Scaffolding has been erected in the middle of the square. Royal court officials are seated in viewing stands, while below on the streets, throngs of commoners press and shove each other, competing for the best line of sight. Guards armed with halberds attempt to keep the ruffians at bay.

The old white horse stops before the raised platform. Quickly, the prisoner is untied from the sled by the attending sentries.

HIE THIS TRAVAIL! screams Edward inside his head. His knees are knocking so severely he cannot walk.

Many in the crowd call out, "COWARD! COWARD!" as Edward is carried under his arms by two soldiers. Waiting at top of the wooden steps is a clergyman, who starts to berate the condemned man about the need to repent. Edward's tongue is a piece of bleeding, mangled muscle. Edward attempts to scream profanities at the priest but can only achieve a garbled spewing of blood followed by a choking fit. Insulted and enraged, the priest turns to the black-hooded executioner and gives the signal for the punishment to proceed. Edward is dragged over to the scaffold.

Wilt ye bargain be honored? Edward keeps asking himself in his state of doom. Is thy hanging to be the agreed end?

A thick loop of rope is secured around Edward's throat by the executioner. On cue, two soldiers take hold of the coil and start hoisting with brute strength. Roars of excitement explode from the crowd as the condemned man is yanked up almost to the top of the crossbeam. Edward kicks out wildly in the air. His neck muscles overstretch and strain. Cervical vertebrae are on the verge of fracturing. The seat of Edward's trousers is soiled darker with a burst of diarrhea. A grey haired, toothless hag, near the bottom of the platform has a tin bowl. She is hoping to collect the condemned man's ejaculation. Edward manages no such arousal. Before his neck bones break, Edward is instantly released from his tether and allowed to plummet back to the floor with a heavy thud.

Edward is motionless. The rough rope has left a painful gash under his chin. Both ankles are sprained from the fall. For a brief moment, Edward has lost consciousness from his carotids being cinched. With the pressure of strangulation gone, he awakes from his grogginess with a sudden, heightened sense of alarm.

DOTH STILL ALIVE! Edward wails internally. 'TWAS PROMISED TO ENDURE NOTHING MORE!

An iron urn of smoldering ash is positioned near the scaffolding. The priest picks up a handful of dried twigs and stokes the embers. He then begins to rant about the fate of traitors being cast into a lake of fire. The clamor from the masses drowns out the priest's tirade. Many in the crowd are panting with sadistic sexual anticipation for the next course of punishment. Lewd jeers are shouted with glee. Two more guards join with the soldiers. The four approach, bend down and take control of each of the condemned man's limbs. Edward thrashes about in vain and is soon held spread-eagle. Lumbering up the creaking wooden steps of the raised platform comes a local Smithfield butcher. He is a tall, baldheaded oaf, wearing a leather apron splattered with dried gore. Besides slaughtering livestock, the butcher is known to geld horses. He is holding a knife. The well-worn blade had just been honed on a grind stone. As the condemned man continues to struggle, the guards yank off his dirty trousers and starkly expose his retracting genitals. The butcher reaches down with a big meaty, scarred hand. Even though the butcher is missing his pinky and half of an index finger, he is still able take hold of the victim's bollocks in a claw-like grip. Choking and sputtering, Edward attempts to scream, "NO! NO!" But all that is heard is more unintelligible gagging. The butcher starts cutting away. Excruciating sharp pain is followed by consuming waves of nausea. Puke shoots up into the back of Edward's mouth. He loses consciousness for a second time as the blood starts to flow. Shrill hoots of elation from the crowd are deafening. The butcher stops, stands and presents to the mob his handful of red dripping family jewels.

"Emasculation and castration!" shouts a magistrate, "Behold ye, wilt assure that a traitor never fathers heirs!" The executioner then orders the butcher to drop the severed privy parts into the burning urn.

Out in the crowd, there is a scraggy young orphan standing on top of a barrel. He is watching with intensity. Clad in rags, he is malnourished and barefoot. His mother was a prostitute that died last year from a bout of the bloody flux. Labeled a bastard child, the lad never knew who was his sire. Continuing to observe the spectacle, he listens to the others around him reveling in enjoyment. Imbued with envy and vengefulness, the poor folk are delighted to see a person of such high social status being treated with substantial cruelty.

Suddenly, a peculiar presence infiltrates the boy's mind. The youth is startled. It makes hissing sounds in his head. The invisible entity whispers to the boy, "Look yonder, nigh the scaffold, behold thy dying father."

Up on the raised platform, Edward jolts to an awaken state. He continues to be held down on his back by the soldiers. Under the filth, his skin is sweaty and ashen. His heart bangs in his heaving chest. The butcher returns to the condemned man to proceed with the evisceration. With a pop, the point of the knife pierces at the navel and works downward through taught abdominal muscles. With care, the butcher makes sure not too slice too deep. Animalistic cries of anguish erupt from Edward, mixing with high-pitched wheezing as he chokes on his own bile.

Another magistrate exclaims, "There shall be no expeditious demise for those who are not loyal to thine majesty! Let such discomfort be lingering!"

Reaching into the incision, the butcher starts to slowly pull out a slippery coil of intestine. Edward shivers uncontrollably. At this catastrophic moment, the entity that dwells among the hedges speaks to him in his mind.

It asks, What is thy offering?

In his crazed torment, Edward replies, All of my soul!

It asks, For how long shall Dudleys be cursed?

Through bloody clenched teeth, Edward snarls, For all time!

It replies, Then I will have thee for all time.

Promptly, Edward's vital pressure drops. His cardiac rhythm is thundering and erratic then abruptly ceases.

To the disappointment of the punishers, Edward gives up the

ghost just as the butcher tugs out another good length of entrails. There is odd silence. All the tortured tension has left Edward's body deflated and seeping. Clouds roll over and the blue sky disappears. The bright sunshine has been extinguished like a candle being snuffed.

The priest announces "Ye traitor's pneuma has left the corporal vessel, but his soul has just been received into Satan's gullet! Burn his black heart to show thine devotion to king and our lord!"

With effort, the butcher starts carving up and under the breastbone. Many times the blade gets stuck as it pokes through the flesh. There is a burst of liquid as the sack around the heart is punctured. The blade scrapes against ribs as it saws about, transecting major arteries. Finally, the heart is retrieved from the body. It is then placed in the urn to be incinerated along with the charring genitals.

Next comes the quartering, as the corpse is dragged over to a chopping block.

A third royal court official stands and exclaims, "Hear ye! Hence, may each limb be displayed in all four corners of thine kingdom as a deterrent for treachery. May his head be placed on a pike at tower bridge!"

The hooded executioner proceeds with the dismemberment. At first, his aim is stellar as he hacks through the right arm with only a few tries from his axe. He does the same with the left. The legs take greater vigor to cut through the large thigh bones. Numerous chops are utilized. The executioner is slick with blood-splatter and perspiration. As the attending solders collect the limbs, they too are red speckled. By the time the executioner is ready for the decapitation he is a bit exhausted. "Boos!" from the crowd are simultaneous as he misses the neck, hits the side of the face, fracturing the jaw and sending fragments of rotting teeth into the air. The second blow, is no better, smashing open the back of the skull. Pink fatty brain tissue dashes across the maroon soaked floor planks. After four more attempts, the head is removed from the carcass in grisly segments.

Dudley's henchman continues to survey among the crowed. They are grateful for the botched disfigurement of the head. The deception is now truly undetectable. Nearby, the young orphan boy remains standing on the barrel, gazing with veneration. The lad's eyes then roll back, showing only the whites as the entity hisses in his mind.

It says to him, "go do thy will in the new world."

***

New World, North America, Quiripipi Tribal Territory August 1623

The temporary encampment is located on the banks of a long winding river aligned with towering pines. Standing near the gate of the stockade, Isabel Dudley is cradling her pregnant belly. She endures another sharp stab of pain as her unborn baby kicks. Grandfather has wandered off again. Her anxiety is great.

She cries aloud, "I shall be scolded for not keeping a watchful eye on thy patriarch!"

Gathering up the helm of her tattered dress, Isabel proceeds to exit the compound. It is a humid hot summer day. There has been no rain for weeks.

"Whence did grandpa stray this time? Oh, how harsh is the brutal sun! Such weather is not favorable for an old man, a woman with child and even thine oxen!" Beads of perspiration roll down from under her bonnet. Sweat stains blotch the fabric under her armpits and between her bosom. Multitudes of mosquitoes frantically buzz about in a haze. The young mother's face and hands are exposed to the frenzy. Pink insect bites dot her clammy white skin.

She slaps a bloated mosquito that attempts to land in the middle of her forehead. She whines, "Hath these furies are relentless! Art thee kin to the plagues that punished the Pharaoh?"

One of the Dutch fur-trappers manning the gate, inquires about the girl's destination.

Isabel addresses the man and sobs, "I was slumbering when I should have been doing thy vigilant duties. What wicked dreams I have! I must find thy grandfather! Surely he could not get far! I do not want to experience the ire of thy mother in-law. She already deems my reputation slothful! Thy husband will surely box thy ears when he returns from his hunt."

The fur-trapper asks with a disrespectful smirk, "So, what did thou dreamt? Was it sinful?"

Quivering, Isabel says, "Thy nightmare was of a little orphan boy standing on a barrel. The lad's eyes were red and yellow-ringed!"

The fur-trapper sneers, "Be same as thou grandfather. He is much a lunatic like most English royals."

***

A bit of distance away from the stockade is an open meadow. The tall dry grass is yellow and brittle. Hunched over and crippled with arthritis, 81-year-old, Abelard Dudley manages to hobble along with his walking stick. Being out in the middle of the field, there is no shade from the glare of the broiling sun. Even though it is now August, he continues to be clad in a heavy coat of pelts. A black, wide-brimmed hat covers his head of wispy white tendrils. Both of his eyes are milky with cataracts, making him see the world in crude extremes of dark and light. There are no teeth left in his lower jaw except for a jagged, tarter-coated incisor.

Drooling, Abelard implores aloud in a croaking voice, "Months ago tither was ice, these days, heat. The temperatures mimic the circles of hell. But thy true torment is thy held water. Please lord, let this pasture be thy chamber pot."

With a shaky hand, he searches for his withered penis through a flap in his trousers. Tugging on the smegma-filled foreskin, Abelard points the tip toward the ground and prays to urinate. A few drops of piss may take an hour to pass. His bladder is dammed and swollen. The ache is maddening and triggers him to ruminate tenfold.

Abelard mutters to himself, "Dear lord, I stand alone in thy open space. I hide not among yonder trees, nor in a cave. I brought thy kin across perilous seas to proceed with a new life. Gladly, I paid these Dutch thieves with much gold to find safe passage in thy wilderness. Some whisper, I am afraid to die because of fear of everlasting damnation. Others, assume I am blessed with old age because I dost like Moses leading thine tribes to the boundaries of Canaan. Every passing day, thou know Lord, I ponder my fate. Dear God, will thou ever answer me? I beseech thee. Wilt I be forgiven for letting a dreg suffer unjust torture and execution for thy welfare? 'Twas all so many years ago."

In the distance, a massive formation of gray clouds is rolling in. Wind rustles through the foreboding forest. The temperature is abruptly dropping as the storm approaches. Suddenly from the edge of the meadow, Abelard's granddaughter appears.

She calls out, "Grandfather! Grandfather! I see thee!"

Abelard is hard of hearing. He does detect her voice and continues to be stooped over in the middle of the meadow, waiting desperately to empty his engorged bladder. The sky directly overhead is now dark. A gust swishes through the dry brittle grass.

"Grandfather, I will take thee by thy arm and guide thee back! 'Tis a hasty tempest that blots out yonder sun!" Isabel begins to waddle forward, her pregnant belly bulging under her dress.

The old man continues to hold his penis. In the following tick of time, there is a brilliant flash in the firmament as a lightning bolt strikes him in the top of head and blows off his wide-brimmed hat. Instantly, the contents of Abelard's skull cooks. Under extreme pressure, liquefied brain tissue squirts out of both ears like hot pink grease. Simultaneously, the large amount of urine in his bladder reaches boiling point. Scalding, steaming piss jets out of Abelard's urethra. The silver buckles on his boots melt into the leather as the energy passes on through to the soil underfoot. A second lightning bolt splinters his arthritic spine and both femurs. The third rapid hit causes the crumpled form of the noble Abelard Dudley to burst into flames. There is no rain with the storm. The meadow of dry brittle grass ignites. Isabel's screams of horror are drowned out by the deafening thunder.

***

Connecticut Colony, Cornwall Township February 1747

The blizzard finally ended on the morning of the Sabbath. Massive snowdrifts are up to the roof of the cabin. Provisions have run out. Gideon Dudley and his family have not eaten in seven days. Wrapped in tattered blankets, they remain huddled around a small hearth. A few wisps of stinging smoke coil in the frigid air. The embers are on the verge of dying out.

Trembling with chills from a fever, Martha moans, "I dreamt of Grandma Isabel last night. She was weeping and warning ye to never eat again."

Stroking her teen-age daughter's sweaty brow, Catherine replies, "Thy grandmother was mad! God rest her soul. Do not listen to such incantations from beyond the grave. Thou are dire for sustenance."

Also stricken with influenza, Gideon coughs and mutters, "The wind has stopped howling. Thanks be to thy Lord that the storm as passed. I wilt go out and forage for food."

Martha whimpers, "No father, thou are ill like me. Thou are in no state to venture out into the woods!"

"Hush child!" snaps Catherine, "Thy father must pull himself to his feet and go hunting, or thou wilt surely die from starvation."

Unexpectedly, little Lydia bursts out from under the fur covers and stands before her kin in an excited state. "Wait!" she exclaims, "I too have dreamt last night!"

The others are a bit shocked to see the child with new born vitality. Eight-year-old Lydia had been disturbingly listless in the past few days. The girl's cheeks are hollow giving her a pronounced skeletal appearance. Now oversized, her linen night dress hangs loosely off her diminutive frame.

Martha cries, "Beloved baby sister, did thou also dream of Grandma Isabel?"

"Nay." giggles Lydia. "Grandma Isabel is buried outside, frozen in nigh coffin."

"Then who did thee dream of?" asks Martha. Lydia answers, "A lad."

"A lad?" inquires Martha.

"Yes, an orphan boy, dressed in rags. His eyes were red and yellow-ringed and shined in yon darkness."

"Stop thy silly banter." scolds Catherine. "Lack of nourishment is causing thy thoughts to be imaginative and strange."

Lydia defies her mother and shouts, "Nay, he is real! And he promised ye a gift!"

"A gift?" Martha responds.

The impish smile drops from Lydia's pale face as she says, "The orphan boy said it is a gift that all Dudley's deserve."

"Cover thee back up under furs before thou catch evil vapors like thine father and sister," orders Catherine. "And be silent! I do not want to hear anymore of thy fanciful tale."

In the next moment, there comes the scent of boiling fish chowder. The aroma permeates through the gaps in the rafters. At first, Catherine assumes that it is fumes from the overflowing chamber pot in the corner of the room but then judges the odor to be pleasant.

"Thou smell that?" Catherine asks her husband.

Congested, Gideon answers, "Nay." He rises on weak legs, clutching his threadbare blanket around his tall gaunt form.

Lydia bolts like a scampering rodent toward the door. The latch miraculously gives way. A surge of wet snow comes spilling across the cabin floor. With a rumble, a section of the drift caves in, instantly creating an ingress. Lydia proceeds to squeeze headfirst into the sloping tunnel. Using her tiny hands, she starts to claw upward.

"What dost possess thy naughty child to be verily?!" hollers Catherine. She tries to catch her daughter by the heel but suffers a kick in the mouth.

"Like a rabbit she is!" says Gideon as he staggers forward. "Catch her, father!" shrieks Martha.

Outside, the light of dawn is hindered by the surrounding hills. Pine boughs droop under the heavy coating of white. A section of the icy mantle shatters as little Lydia burrows up to the surface. She pokes out, waist deep in the hole. A few paces away, stuck in the snow is a large iron pot. Its contents are hot and bubbling. Rising steam spreads the potent scent.

Lydia gasps as she sees the gift.

"Come hither! Come hither!" screeches Lydia with elation.

Applying great effort, mother and father dig a passage. They join their daughter at the top of the snow mound.

Shivering, Lydia cries, "Behold, Father! Behold!" She points out toward the brewing vessel.

"Doth witchcraft be involved?" says Catherine with alarm. Taking his dirty thumb and pressing the side of his nose, Gideon blows hard. Mucus bursts from his left nostril. With a glob of yellow-greenish snot hanging from his straggly beard, Gideon smiles as he breathes in deep. The symptoms of influenza immediately subside. After a pause, he then proclaims, "I have just been able to detect cooking of chowder! 'Tis a welcomed fragrance indeed!"

With brows knitted, Catherine petitions her husband, "Thou art dreadfully famished, but yonder gift is peculiar! I see no footprints in much snow!"

Gideon answers, "Maybe it was dropped hence like manna from heaven! Could Indians be the purveyors? Savages knowest to cover thine tracks."

"Nay!" cries the little Lydia, "I told ye it is a bequest from the orphan boy!"

"So be it!" retorts Gideon with frustration, "I care not who is the true gift-bearer! There is a lid covering yon vessel. I just pray that the substances of that pot are as savory as the alluring redolence! Woman, gather thine spoons while I dost retrieve this bounty!"

The man takes labored strides as he struggles through the deep snow toward the pot. More than once, Gideon burns his hands on the sizzling iron as he attempts to drag the vessel home.

Inside the cabin, Martha's illness also vanishes. There is a commotion as her parents and little sister toil back through the partially clogged doorway. Her appetite rebounds as she sees the steaming pot being jostled and pushed up next to the hearth. Martha cries, "Father, are ye saved? What is in thy crock? Has God answered ye desperate prayers?"

"Ye shall see!" replies Gideon as he blisters his fingers again while quickly lifting off the lid and letting it drop. The hot metal cover makes a hissing sound as it lands on the slush-covered floor. Humid steam bellows out from the pot and is temporarily blinding. As the vapors dissipate, the contents of the vessel are revealed.

"Oh, how I yearned for such victuals!" exclaims Gideon with astonishment.

The pot is brimming with clams, crabs, mussels, and various fish. A whole lobster is the star ingredient in the broth. Chunks of brat ruben float on top of the broth which is spiked with Malmsey wine.

"Whence dost gifts from distant seas travel here?" Queries Catherine, "Ye are afar inland!"

Lydia speaks up in a shrill voice, "Thy orphan boy told I in thy dreams that he netted all things in the pot from waters nigh his village."

"Do tell. Whence village?" asks Martha. "Milford," peeps Lydia.

Gideon says, "As I stated before, I care not to ponder the source of this gift! I am too ravished to contemplate a mystery. Let ye eat! It is thy command!"

Obediently, Catherine quickly gathers wooden bowls and spoons for all. She ladles out the fish stew and serves it to her daughters first.

Gideon declares, "Eat ye children! How I feared all would die as if stricken by the rider on the black horse of famine!"

Preparing her husband's dish, Catherine solicits, "Shall thou pause and say grace?"

"Thy will pray as thy consume!" barks Gideon. Ignoring the piping hot temperature, the man begins to snatch pieces of fish straight from the pot and stuffing them in his mouth. Next, he grabs the half open clams to gnaw out the morsels. With a sudden loss of manners, he tosses the empty shells over his shoulder and continues to repeat the same action but with accelerating intensity. A few of the clam shells bounce off Martha's bonnet.

Going against her intuition, Catherine takes a sip of broth.

Immediately, her own state of hunger is awakened. Her motherly vigilance evaporates. Possessed with a sudden crazed urge to gorge, she too starts to slurp and gulp down the contents of her bowl. Catherine fails to notice that little Lydia is not eating but rather standing stiffly in a trance.

Martha is also taken over with the drive to feast. The teenage girl greedily sucks on the head of a sea bass and uses the tip of her tongue to get every salty tidbit. She is distracted and unaware that her little sister's eyes are rolling back in her skull, displaying only the ghostly whites.

Father lifts out the lobster. There is a sharp cracking sound as he bites down hard through one of its claws. He swallows the lobster meat and shell together with gusto. Next, he pulls open the thorax and gobbles away. Continuing to dismantle the crustacean, he chomps through the tail's exoskeleton. Jagged fragments of lobster shell pierce his tongue.

Becoming more untamed, Catherine and Martha are up to their elbows as they reach into the vessel to retrieve more nutriments. Abandoning spoons and bowls, they too eat with their hands and endure burns to both fingers and lips. Gideon pushes the women away and impulsively dunks his whole head into the pot to guzzle the broth. Almost drowning, his wife grabs him by his long greasy hair and pulls him back up. Gideon's face is coated and dripping with scalding stew. A whole porgy is clenched sideways between his damaged teeth. With no intelligible words exchanged, the three snarl, grunt and continue to compete for the fruta del mar.

No one observes that little Lydia's eyes have turned pure black.

It is when the iron pot is two-thirds empty that the veil of deception is lifted. Rather the vessel being a cornucopia of fresh catch from the sea, it suddenly morphs into a cauldron of decay and poison. The fish in the pot and in the Dudley's bellies is now rancid and teaming with aquatic parasites. A putrid stench of rotting marine fauna is suffocating in the small confines of the cabin. The stew's broth is infused with azaspiracid toxins, botulinum and cholera.

Excruciating stomach cramps causes Catherine to instantly double over. Rapid incubation of vulnificus infiltrates her guts along with a horde of tapeworms. Martha screams as long thin fish bones come poking through her cheeks like prickly needles. At this very moment, the teenager is stricken with an infection of vibrio alginolyticus. Pink froth spews from her mouth as she thrashes about with a grand mal seizure. Gideon Dudley's esophagus is lacerated and flayed as he regurgitates the shards of lobster shells in a forceful jet of scarlet. Thousands of wiggly nematodes are already marauding into the ventricles of his brain. The snow-covered floor of the cabin is turning into a slushy mix of gore and vomitus.

Little Lydia turns and slowly departs as her family writhes in torment. Outside, she is impervious to the cold. She plods barefoot through the deep drifts of white in a catatonic slumber. A wintery gust flutters the child's linen night dress. Her irises have become red and yellow-ringed. The dense snowy forest beckons. Noises resonate from the cabin, as the frigid wind carries the mingled groans of agony up into the trees.

***

Connecticut Colony, Cornwall Township March 1747

Barzallai Dudley has been praying for the day to unite with his brother Gideon. The journey has taken months. Melting snows have given the arriving party an arduous slog through the mud. The bright blue clear sky is obstructed by the three encircling hills, casting the area with a somber shade.

Up ahead in a small clearing, the wooden cabin comes into view. There is no smoke emitting from the chimney nor signs of lively habitation. The small wooden dwelling appears weather-worn and foreboding. Where there once was a front door, now there is none. It is off it's hinges and has collapsed inward.

"Thank thee, Dear Lord God!" shouts Barzallai. "Finally thy destination reached! Brother, can thou hear me?" Barzallai dismounts from his horse with excitement. He addresses his two teenage sons and says, "Attend to thy mother while I summon Gideon and thine family!"

Cradling her belly and huffing with discomfort, Rachael makes it off the back of the ox-pulled cart. Horace and James had taken her hand. She is seven months pregnant and weary of travel. Shuffling away from her boys, Rachael searches for a thicket to squat behind and piss.

On his way toward the cabin, Barzallai's fervor impedes his awareness of the menacing deadness of the environment. The stink wafting from the dwelling has not yet triggered a sense of danger. "Rejoice! Rejoice?" calls Barzallai. "Where art thy greeters?

How shall ye celebrate? Hello, where art thou?"

Only when he reaches the entrance to the cabin is his joy extinguished. Barzallai's physical self instantly becomes immobile while his mental faculties are stricken with nightmarish vertigo. The odor is hideous. Reflexively, he swallows back his puke. Peering in from the doorway, it was difficult to discern the bodies in the darkness. Decomposition has only recently hastened with the thawing temperatures of the approaching spring. Laying supine on the floor boards, Martha's facial features are those of a rotting skull but her nude carcass is still quite fleshy. The girl's dermis is multicolored with black spidery lividity and bluish-ochre blotches. Sludge leaks out between Martha's legs. Live cod worms slither about in her putrefying virgin womb.

Nearby, Catherine's corpse is positioned in a grotesque pose. She is head down, torso tilted forward on bent knees. Her moldering grey dress and under garments are bunched up around her mid-section. Obscenely, her exposed buttocks are pointing upward. Pelvic bones are starting to jut through the sloughing grey flesh.

When Barzallia sees Gideon's corpse, he manages a gasping sob, "D-D- Dearest brother!"

Gideon is slumped against the far wall. His corroding face is streaked with umber. Mice have eaten through his eye sockets. In the corpse's lap is a hairy mass encrusted with dried blood and skin. A sharp piece of clam shell is still clutched between his skeletal fingers. Gideon had scalped himself in his final throes of insanity.

Suddenly the unnerving silence is broken by clicking and tapping. The sound is coming from inside the dirty iron pot. With his will completely controlled, Barzallia finds himself walking stiffly into the cabin. He approaches the pot, stops and stares down. The very bottom of the vessel is coated with congealed muck. It is all that remains of the poisoned stew. Something scurries about on the surface of the left-overs. A tiny spider crab taps the side of the pot again with its claw. It is demanding Barzallia's attention. Telepathically, the crab hisses and whispers in Barzallia's mind,

"Thou request knowledge of what smite thine brother, sister in-law and fare nieces?"

With is his pulse pounding like war drums, Barzallia replies with trembling fear, "Ney, I cannot bear to learn such malevolence!"

The entity hisses louder and scolds, "Coward! Then thou shall witness a mere glimpse!"

Hellish images abruptly manifest in Barzallia's brain. Catherine is bending over as blue-green projectile diarrhea explodes from her anus like grape shot from a blunder buster. The amoeba- infected feces splatters the rafters and then drips down on all occupants in the cabin. The next flashback reveals Martha tearing off her linens while convulsing. Blood and fish scales burst from her mangled mouth as a wet glittery discharge. Gideon is laughing like a lunatic and singing church hymns as he runs the shard of clam shell vertically up his forearm creating a deep spurting gash.

Horace is approaching the cabin when he hears his father's ear-splitting cry. In the next moment, Barzallia comes bursting out the doorway. The father shoves his son in the chest and screams, "I forbid thee to go in there! Go retrieve the lamp oil and kindling!"

"What do thou ask? I don't understand!" Horace shouts. Barzallia roars, "Do as I say or I will curse thee!"

Down near the cart, Rachael hears the commotion. The pack animals are spooked. Suddenly, Barzallia's horse rears up on its back legs, neighing loudly in panic. The mare then comes back down to all fours and bolts. It is headed for the forest.

"James, retrieve thy father's mount!" shrieks Raphael.

Oddly pan-faced, James turns and begins walking toward the

forest with no display of urgency.

Shaking, Rachael addresses Horace, her eldest son, as he starts gathering items from the wagon in haste. She bawls, "Dost Indians massacre thine kin? What reason thou father be so troubled?"

"I know not!" Horace shouts at his mother. "Father demands such to make a fire!"

" 'Tis the plague?" Rachael wails.

Horace does not answer but rather races back to join his father. Frantically, Barzallia keeps striking a piece of flint. Hands trembling, his skills to create a spark is greatly impaired.

Crouching down, next to his father, Horace offers a patch of cloth soaked with oily tallow. After the hundredth attempt, there is ignition of the rag.

***

Bright orange flames proceed to consume the cabin as evening arrives. Flickering light creates gyrating shadows that disturb the surrounding dark forest. Periodically, a putrid whiff of diseased broiling meat makes the observers nauseous.

Huddled near the oxen cart with husband and son, Rachael has not stopped weeping. She finally speaks her mind and blurts, "This is not a proper Christian burial!"

Since starting the fire, Barzarllia has not uttered a word. Withdrawn and unblinking, his once jolly face is now blackened with soot. Sitting with his back against the wagon wheel, he quietly picks grit from his fingernails.

Horace had gone out looking for his brother but since returned at dusk.

Shaking with emotion, Rachael petitions, "Please my husband. Please Horace. I beseech thee! Keep praying for James' safe passage back to us. Please don't pause in thy prayers for even a single moment as we wait here in vigil."

"Worry not, mother." Horace replies, "I will not stop my prayers and at dawn I shall continue my search into the wilderness."

Blunted, Barzallia says nothing and continues to gaze into space.

Inside the cabin, the timbers are charring and being incinerated with oxygen-rich flames. The iron pot is now glowing white-hot. Bones of the dead sizzle, pop and fragment. The burning floorboards finally crumble, and the pot drops downward into a small root cellar. Simultaneously, the rafters give way and the roof collapses with a burst of flames shooting into the night sky. Floating orange sparks threaten the nearby brush. Downwind, the three endure bellowing stinging smoke.

Rachael coughs then blubbers, "Woe to such calamity!" She hugs her pregnant belly in despair.

A single tear shines in Barzallia's left eye.

Suddenly there is the whinnying of a horse and the rustling of branches. James slowly comes into view on horseback. Both boy and beast are silhouetted as they pause in front of the conflagration.

"THANKS BE TO GOD!" exclaims Rachael. Horace immediately helps his mother to her feet. Father stays seated while the two rush toward James. Upon approaching, Rachael cries "Come down from thy father's mount and embrace thy mother!"

Horace takes hold of the bridle and laughs, "Hello thy younger brother! How did thee tame this charger!"

Strangely vacant of emotion, James stays seated on the horse. He replies coldly, "A little orphan boy in the woods led me to thy mare."

"Get down from thy horse!" orders Rachael. "All must attend to thine father. He is stricken with melancholia. By morning light, we shall pack up and depart this wicked place!"

James replies, "None are allowed to leave here." "Thou jest," says Horace, "Ye are to make haven at this very spot," says James. There   is an unnerving, detached quality to his speech. He states, "All Dudley's will be summoned here."

James then begins to gag. His brother and mother assume he is bothered by the drifting smoke. The youth coughs up a thing from his stomach and into his palm. Using its tiny claw, the thing pinches James' finger. It is the spider crab that had escaped from the iron pot.

***

Cornwall, Connecticut May 1880

Agnes spits, "That is your last tug, swine!"

"Damn whore!" the reverend curses as he stuffs his softening member back into his trousers. "This is as far as we go. Get out of your seat and be gone with you!"

Agnes steps down from the carriage as the reverend cracks a

whip on the rump of his nag. The horse and buggy pulls away, leaving the woman standing alone on the side of a dirt road. The unscrupulous reverend had agreed to give Agnes a ride in exchange for frequent deviant attention. Traveling from the coast, the trip had taken more than a week. Along the way, they often stayed in barns during the night. Agnes deplored those horrible evenings. The reverend assumed that Agnes was a harlot fleeing the brutality of some brothel. He had first discovered her wandering alone on a wagon path in Milford. In actuality, Agnes was never a prostitute but rather a ward of the institute for the insane. The hissing and whispering had gotten worse over the last year. As spring arrived, a particularly forceful voice had commanded her to escape the asylum and to find Dudley Town.

With a resigned sigh, Agnes proclaims to herself, "Like little Red Riding Hood, I must now follow this ascending path into the woods. I fear no wolf because it is where my secret guide tells me to go. It is my destiny. How magnificent will this village be?"

With her palm sticky, Agnes wipes the repulsive essence on the bark of a birch tree and proceeds with her journey. A short distance away, the lonely dirt road is the trailhead. The route quickly turns steep. Dense forests align the way. Agnes perspires in her frayed dress and dirty bloomers. It is not long before painful blisters form on both her heels. The woman's old leather shoes are no match for the rocky ground. Newly hatched mosquitoes begin to gather in a frenzy. Soon Agnes's moist pale skin is dotted with insect bites.

Swatting away, she hollers, "You pests may sting me, but you are still not as loathsome as that damn reverend! I rather endure your molestation than his!"

Undeterred, Agnes treks up the winding incline. She smiles despite the ache. Once again, she is fantasizing about finding paradise. Agnes has daydreamed about this ever since those days in the orphanage. Breathing heavily, she mutters, "Will Dudley Town be my new home? Will there be apple orchards; pie bakers; blueberry jam makers; honey bees; kittens; kites; butterflies; laughing children; jolly grannies; beautiful flowers..."

Almost an hour passes. With a couple of more laborious steps, she reaches the top of the plateau.

The entity mocks Agnes. It snickers in her mind and says, "Behold utopia."

Stunned and short of breath, Agnes questions aloud, "I-I-I don't understand! Where is the town?"

Three tall hills block the natural light of day. Even though it is noon, it appears like dusk. Stone walls mark the parameter of an abandoned settlement. A few empty houses have been left to deteriorate in the somber desolation. The wooden structures are gray and weathered. Dead leaves from numerous autumns have blown in through open windows and covered the interiors with drifts of mulch. Black mold infects the dwelling's buckling walls. The livestock pens are empty and scattered with old bone fragments. An unnerving silence envelopes the area. There is not the single chirp of a bird nor the rustle of wind. Even the hungry mosquitoes have vanished.

For a moment, Agnes can only hear her rapid pulse pounding in her ears. She then whimpers aloud, "Why-Why did you lead me here?"

After a pause, the entity hisses in her mind and replies, "To crush your hope."

With tears streaming down her checks, Agnes nods in resignation. She sobs, "too good to be true."

The entity says, "You deserve no joy."

Agnes abruptly stops crying. She then notices an oak tree near a stone wall. One of its branches is low hanging. Agnes kicks off her old leather shoes. She next pulls down her bloomers and ties the garment around her waist like a sash. The woman approaches the stonewall and gets on top. She makes her way to the low lying bough. Propelled by an odd force, Agnes begins to climb. The entity has bestowed its host with a primate-like agility. Higher and higher, Agnes scales the mighty oak. Soon her greasy auburn hair becomes undone from its ribbon. Being scratched and poked by branches are not deterrents. Crawling out on a high tree limb, Agnes steadies herself as she loops one leg of the bloomer around the bough. She then ties the other end of the garment around her neck. Without the slightest hesitation she lets herself tumble off into space. For a fleeting few seconds the noose holds. Her legs kick wildly as she dangles in mid air. Agnes gags, sputters, and pisses. Suddenly there is a loud cracking sound as the bough breaks. The tree limb plummets along with the Agnes's tethered body. It is a ten-foot drop. All comes crashing down into a heap.

The unnatural silence returns as the echo fades. A moment passes.

With eyelids flickering, Agnes starts to regain consciousness.

Immediately she is stricken with a sense of panic. She screams in her mind, "Why am I still alive! The hanging was supposed to be my end!"

A pointy segment of fractured fibula juts out of her left calf muscle. Both ankles are broken as well as the woman's right arm. She does not feel the pain of her injuries because of a partially severed spinal cord. Immobility is from the neck down. Gulping for air, Agnes is lying on her side with her left ear pressed to the earth.

"What happened to me?" she wails in her mind.

Underneath Agnes, in a hollow space in the ground, comes the sound of bubbling. At first it is muffled and faint but is now pronounced. Agnes catches a whiff of fish chowder in her nostrils. Next, up on the surface, there are approaching footsteps and the rustle of a branch stick being dragged along.

A child's voice asks, "Can thy hear ye pot boiling from yonder root cellar?"

It is impossible for Agnes to turn her head and to observe the source of the voice. Nor is Agnes able to detect her rump being prodded with the branch stick.

With a taunting tone, the child giggles, "Doest know me? Nay?"

From her helpless position, Agnes awaits. The child steps around to the front. Peering up in horror, Agnes wants to scream but can only manage a wheezing gurgle.

Little Lydia is still clad in her tattered night dress. Withered brown jerkin barely covers her skeleton. A few wisps of hair remain on her thin scalp. Her nose and lips have rotted away, leaving a grimacing skull. One eyeball remains in the socket. The sclera is black, and the iris is red and yellow-ringed.

Little Lydia glares down at Agnes and states in a sweet manner, "Thy grannie was Rachael Dudley. I smote her and thy mother."

Agnes emits a high-pitched groan.

As if kicking a ball with great enthusiasm, little Lydia boots the side of Agnes's head with her tiny skeletal foot. The last strands of Agnes's cervical spinal cord detach.

The silence returns accept for the faint bubbling of the iron pot under the earth.

***

Cornwall, Connecticut August 1967

"Hey, did you notice there is no sound of birds?" asks Bill. "I don't hear anything, not even one cricket," replies Mary. "Sure you want to stay alone here tonight?"

Mary gives a weak smile and answers, "My shrink says that I need to be more comfortable with solitude."

Uneasy, Bill sighs, "Well, if you want seclusion, this is the place." again."

"It is nice to be away from the city. Maybe I can start writing "That would be good. Out in the woods, penning the next Walden's Pond."

"I'm just a bit worried about Nathaniel."

Bill touches his wife's shoulder, "Nat is safe with my folks.

They're probably spoiling the hell out of him right now." Mary hugs her husband and says, "I love you."

"I feel guilty leaving you here." Bill squeezes her tightly.

Mary attempts to make light of the situation. "Well, that's what happens when a girl marries a doctor."

"I promise to finish my work at the hospital and be back tomorrow afternoon to start our romantic vacation in the great outdoors! Are you angry with me? Tell me the truth. You are not going to leave me for some beatnik poet?"

She teases, "Are you getting obsessive like your brother?" Bill laughs, "I still can't believe that John made it through the police academy. He was such a hooligan as a teenager. The mayhem he caused in Milford is unforgiveable. Now he's a constable!"

"He sure is an odd duck."

"Yes, indeed. But not to sound neurotic, are you truly okay with being alone in the dark?"

"I'm prepared like a good girl scout. I have my flashlight. I got my lantern. I will be toasting marshmallows at midnight around the campfire."

"Well, try not to burn down the forest."

"Okay, Smokey the Bear," Mary quips. She then hugs her husband again and tries to be reassuring. "Go quick. See your patients. And don't worry about me."

"You're the best."

The two walk down the path to the main road. They say their last good-byes. Waving and honking, Bill departs in their Buick station wagon. As soon as Mary starts walking back to the camp site, a swarm of mosquitoes attack.

"Ouch, damn it!" she slaps at her neck and arms.

Once Mary makes it up to the plateau the insects quickly disappear. Even though it is three in the afternoon, the bright sunlight is blocked by the surrounding hills. The forest is dreary. There is an unnatural stillness. Near the campsite there are meandering old stone walls. Green moss coats the rocks. The houses and barns have since decayed and collapsed. Heaps of ancient rotting wood fill the crumbled foundations. A gnarled oak tree stands in the middle of the clearing like a monstrous sentinel, its twisting branches are black and leafless; scratching her. Mary is struck with a sudden sense of desolation. Her stomach starts to rumble. It is a nauseating feeling, similar to the time when she ate bad clams. She gripes to herself, "Now I know why my kin fled this place? Melancholia must have been rampant. What the heck was I thinking when I told Bill I wanted to come here?"

***

The last embers in the campfire die out as midnight passes. Mary is doubled over in the tent, clenching her belly and shivering. She had regurgitated chunks of hotdog and six toasted marshmallows. Desperately, she prays for the nausea to cease and for the night to end. Never before has Mary felt this vulnerable. Nearby on the soiled blanket is her new journal book. All the pages are blank.

Ever so slightly, out in the darkness, the silence is broken by the sound of bubbling. It is coming from underneath one of the old foundations. Next, there is the rustling of branches. Someone is approaching from the woods.

Mary shudders, "Who's there?" The jolt of fear gives her the energy to rise up and peer out the tent flap. With trembling hands, she shines the flashlight into the blackness. The jittery beam dances about. A scream erupts from her mouth as a quick glimpse of a naked figure is caught in the illumination. It is an older boy. He is bone thin and bald. Every single strand of hair as been singed from his pale, emaciated body. Gory essence still remains congealed on his face and arms from over two hundred years ago. It is his sire's blood. The boy had dropped a 70-pound field stone on his father's head. Barzallia was sleeping when his skull was crushed in.

"W-Who-Who are you?" Mary whimpers in terror. With a hiss the boy replies, "James Dudley."

The boy's sclera is black like squid ink. His iris's are red and orange ringed.

***

The next evening, Bill speeds along rural back roads. He is late and a bit lost. The plan was to return in the early afternoon but he was caught at the hospital with an emergency delivery. It was a breech birth. Tragically, the infant died. On the passenger seat of the Buick are a dozen wilting red roses, a bottle of warm champagne and a property deed. Bill attends to surprise Mary with the land purchase.

They both dreamed of having a country hideaway. He can't wait to see the look of joy on her face. The parcel is the exact spot where her ancestors once established a town. For Bill, it has been a bitter sweet day full of sadness, anxiety and anticipation. He drives faster.

"Damn, where is the turn off!" Bill curses, "Did I miss it again?"

There are no street lights out in the rolling expanses of farmland. At night, everything looks the same. Bill travels on, finally coming to a narrow strip of dirt road aligned with black pines. Zooming around a curve, he catches a glimpse of a figure on the embankment. It is a little girl dressed in rags. Her eyes shine red and orange.

"Who is that?" Bill says aloud. He keeps driving. He then mutters, "Weird. Maybe I'm seeing things."

Bill finally notices the entrance point to the campsite. He barrels up the dirt pathway. The Buick's headlights pierce through the dense woods. Hitting ruts and rocks, Bill decides to stop the vehicle before blowing a tire. In haste, he stuffs the land deed into his jacket pocket. He leaves the flowers and champagne behind. Flashlight in hand, Bill hoofs it the rest of the way. The mosquitoes attack like furies. Undeterred, Bill makes it to the plateau.

"Mary! Mary! I'm here!" Bill shouts. His voice echoes in the blackness.

The campsite appears abandoned.

Instantly, Bill is concerned. He expected to find a roaring campfire and his beloved wife rushing into his arms.

"Mary are you sleeping? Mary!"

Bill hurries to the tent and pushes aside the flap. The lantern is unlit. There is the stink of dried vomit. Bill's flashlight shines on the soiled blanket. He catches sight of her open journal book.

Scrawled across a page is the message, "This time the bough did not break." signed Mary Dudley.

"What is this?" Bill is stunned.

He quickly exits the tent to search the area.

"MARY! MARY!" Bill yells, "WHERE ARE YOU?"

He frantically scans about with his flashlight. "MARY ANSWER ME?"

Bill's desperate calls resonate in the eerie silence. "Did she leave me?" Bill gasps.

The flashlight beam illuminates a portion of the stone walls then out toward the woods. Bill approaches near the old oak tree and catches a whiff of something foul. He shines the light on the ground. A small pile of dead leaves is splattered with coagulated diarrhea and blood. In the next second, a droplet of thick mucus falls from above and hits Bill on the top of his head.

"What the hell!" Bill does a startled jump.

Instantly he shines the flashlight up into the oak tree. High above from a jutting bough, Mary's lifeless body hangs by the neck. Quietly, the big branch creaks as the corpse gently sways. The material from her bell bottom jeans had been torn asunder and crudely knotted into a noose. She is naked from the waist down. Something drops from her womb. It lands on Bills lapel and latches on with its tiny claw. It is the spider crab. Bill instinctually flicks it away as he screams in utter madness and despair.

***

Cornwall Connecticut Present day

It is a grey morning. Drizzle beads on the windows. Kate wakes up with nausea and rushes to the bathroom to regurgitate. The lights on the vanity are harsh. She looks at herself in the mirror. There are dark circles under her eyes.

"Can't live like this anymore." She cries as she dabs the puke off her chin with quilted scented bath tissue. Gotta be strong.

Enough is enough. I have to confront him!

Nathanial did not come to bed last night. Again he spent the whole time in the den transfixed in front of the computer. Kate regrets ever buying her husband that DNA ancestry kit.

Clutching her bathrobe around her body, she gingerly walks down the carpeted hallway. Swallowing hard, she pauses outside the doorway to the den. Kate knocks.

No reply.

She taps again. Nothing.

Taking a deep breath, Kate opens the door. "Nathanial?"

Hunched behind the monitor, her husband does not look up. It has been over two weeks and Nathanial is still wearing the same clothes. His yellow I-Zod short sleeve shirt and plaid golf pants are gamey and stained. Greasy cowlicks stick up from the middle of his head. He is unshaven with blotchy stubble. Dozens of empty coffee cups are strewn about the cluttered den.

Irritated and scared, Kate barks, "Nate, why are you not answering me?"

Startled, Nathanial breaks his gaze from the computer and looks up at his wife with blood-shot eyes. He stutters, "Oh, I-I didn't see you standing there."

"My god, what's happening to you? You promised you were going to get some sleep!"

Clearing his dry throat, Nathanial says, "My father lied to me. My mother didn't die in a car accident. She committed suicide."

"Huh?" Kate gasps. "What are you talking about?"

"I have been doing so much research. The police report from 1967 says she hung herself in the woods outside."

"I don't believe it! That's terrible! Where are you getting this information from? What website?"

"My dad never wanted me to have this property. That's why he never mentioned owning it."

"Nonsense! You know he lost his capability to remember stuff."

"Why was he always screaming about crabs?"

"He was psychotic. Dementia can cause someone to be delusional. The poor man was constantly talking gibberish. He was 95 years old!"

"The ancestry test indicated I am a Dudley. I have been researching all Dudleys. It's a cursed royal blood line. My mother was a Dudley. The curse pulls us back here."

Kate's face turns red with frustration. Tears burst down her checks. She cries, "Stop it! Inheriting this property and building our dream house in the woods is a beautiful blessing, not a curse. The reality is, you're having a nervous breakdown! You have been depressed for over a year since your father's death. Seeing him deteriorate with Alzheimer's was horrific. You need to get some goddamn help!"

Nate stares back at his wife with a quivering lower lip. He mutters, "This land is my killing ground."

"Bullshit!" Kate yells. She points a finger at her husband. "Listen, the only thing dangerous around here is Lyme Disease.

Maybe you got it. I heard tick bites can effect your brain! It too can cause depression. Last summer, you did have a bull's eye rash on your leg."

Nate appears stupefied.

"I need you to go to a doctor for a complete check-up. You're not working, and the bills are piling up. You're not even bathing anymore. You stink! And you're believing crazy shit!"

Slowly, Nathanial turns his gaze back to the computer screen. Dialing down her anger, Kate pleads, "Stop shutting me out, honey! I don't want to be mean. I'm just so worried about you.

Where is the fun-loving guy that I used to know? The one that played golf and enjoyed puttering in the yard."

Nate is silent.

Kate exhales loudly. "Listen, I have my own doctor's appointment this morning. I haven't been feeling right either. Hope by the time I come home you will at least have taken a shower."

Nate does not respond.

Kate sobs loudly as she turns to leave. She slams the door to the den. Nate is again solitary in the cluttered little room. A small amount of time passes. Through the walls he listens to his wife getting ready. Next, comes the sound of her speeding away in their Volvo station wagon.

Finally, he is alone in the house. More moments tick by. A faint bubbling sound comes reverberating up from the cellar. Nathanial rises from his chair and folds over the braided throw rug. Going down on all fours, he presses his ear to the wooden floor plank.

He whispers, "Something is cooking deep below under the house." He then sniffs the air and asks aloud, "Could it be chowder?"

Inside one of the dirty coffee mugs, something starts tapping with its tiny claw. Nathanial gets back up and steps over to the desk. Peering down into the coffee mug he sees the spider crab. Telepathically, the crustacean hisses in Nathanial's mind. It tells Nathanial to go into the woods. With no hesitation, Nathanial does an about-face and leaves the den. He does not pause to put on his shoes. Nathanial proceeds across the backyard in his socks. The ground is soggy and layered with decaying autumn leaves. Climbing over a portion of the old stone walls, he proceeds into the forest. The cool damp air seems to shock him out of his trance. High above, a patch of blue sky peaks through the grey clouds. A beam of happy sunlight shines on Nathanial's haggard face. He is standing next to the ancient oak. Unknown to him, it is the same tree where his mother hung from a bough. The core of the gnarled oak is rotten and hallow. Nathanial basks in the sunshine and is suddenly imbued with a wonderful feeling of wellness.

"Wow, I feel so good!" he exclaims. "What just happened?"

Nathanial is suddenly reminded of the story of clarity being obtained under the boughs of the Ficus religiosa. He begins to laugh hysterically. He exclaims aloud, "Did I just achieve fucking enlightenment? What was I thinking this whole time? Kate is right! The curse is a bunch of bullshit! It's fucking folklore! Everything is explainable. Lightening kills. Eating bad shell fish can be fatal! Cabin fever can cause someone to go nuts! People commit suicide everyday. It's stuff that happens all the time. There is nothing paranormal about any of it!"

In the next moment, the patch of blue sky is engulfed by the somber clouds. The sunlight is extinguished from Nathanial's jubilant face.

The entity hisses in his brain, "A silver lining for a Dudley.

Tis not allowed."

The joy in Nathanial's heart is turned off like a switch.

"Oh God!" Nathanial whimpers as he clutches his chest. "The depression is back!"

There is the rustling of branches as something big comes charging from the woods. Usually an adult black bear weighs 240 pounds but this animal is underweight due to intestinal tapeworms. Famished and rabid, it attacks. Nathanial screams as he is plowed over onto his side. The bear latches onto his defensive forearm and begins to viscously shake its huge head. Nathanial's ulna fractures as his humerus dislocates from the socket shoulder. The bear lets go. Frantically, Nathanial kicks up with his legs. Swipes from the animal's claws shreds his golf pants and gouges the flesh underneath.

The bear lunges down and takes hold of the man's inner thigh. Nathanial pounds on top of the beast's skull with one fist.

"Get off me! Get the fuck off me! Fuck! HELP!"

Yellowed fangs pierce deep and nick the femoral artery. With a red spurt, over a pound of flesh is pulled from the bone. Nathanial screeches in agony. The bear bites down again, this time gorging on Nathanial's crotch.

"AHHHHHHH!"

In a nightmarish frenzy, Nathanial is emasculated and suffers a lacerated bladder. Perineal muscle and a flap of scrotum become entangled with strips of plaid cloth and a trouser zipper. The bloody wad gets momentarily stuck in the animal's throat. With hacking burst, the bear spits out the obstruction. Racked with nauseating vertigo, Nathanial is rolled onto his belly. Teeth jab through his scalp followed by vice like-pressure on his cranium. The bear abruptly stops gnawing on his head. Nathaniel is tossed aside. For a second, he gazes up into the bear's eyes. The animal's sclera is black. Its irises are red and orange-ringed. Nathaniel wants to continue to wail but can only manage a fading groan as he goes into shock.

The entity hisses, "Thy will be done."

The coup de grass is the drooling fanged-jaws clamping around Nathaniel's throat. The bear rips and tears away at its listless prey. A massive, gaping neck wound leaves Nathaniel nearly decapitated.

***

Speeding toward home through the rural back roads, Kate is an emotional jumble of elation and dread. Two months ago, she forced Nathaniel to be intimate. Void of passion, he came in less than a minute and went back on the computer. Kate is confounded how that joyless encounter resulted in her getting knocked-up. She keeps wondering if the news of being a father will pop Nathaniel out of his funk or send him further over the edge. They never planned to have children. She just turned 40 and Nate is in his 50's. The results from the pregnancy test are stuffed in her purse. The doctor confirmed it.

"Now I know why I kept puking every morning!" Kate zooms up the steep driveway to the house.

"I have to be brave! I have to be strong!" She keeps coaching herself.

Kate parks the Volvo and hurries up the stone walkway, purse in hand. A Zeka infected mosquito lands on her cheek and injects its labium. She swats it away. As Kate enters the house, she winces from the ear-splitting clamor. The big screen Samsung is on. The speakers from elaborate surround sound system are cranked to the max.

"Why is the television so loud?"

Breaking news about a gruesome murder in Milford Connecticut comes blaring. There are images of a sailboat stuck on a sandbar. Charles Island flashes across the TV screen. Kate frantically searches the nearby recliner for the remote. Silence abruptly envelopes the home as she turns off the television.

"What was that all about?" she exclaims.

Taking a deep breath, Kate then calls out, "Nate? Where are you? Hello?"

No response.

She quickly walks down the hall to the den. Kate opens the door expecting to find her husband glued in front of the monitor. He is not there. She wrinkles her nose as she catches a whiff of rotting fish.

"What's that smell? Yuck!"

Something tiny scurries across the floor boards and into the corner.

"What was that? A crab?" Kate is unnerved.

At that very moment, the entity whispers in the woman's mind, "Mother to be, go ye search in yonder forest."

Trembling Kate gasps, "What was that voice? Who just said that?"

A chilling breeze makes the door to the sun porch creak on its hinges. Kate rushes over to discover that it is wide open. She exits the house and crosses the backyard. Dirtying her skirt, she climbs over the mossy stone wall.

With fear in her voice, she shrieks, "Nate? Where are you? Nate?" Her cries echo in the desolation.

Moving deeper into the woods. She comes to the gnarled oak tree. There are strong mixed odors in the air: animal urine; human blood; wet earth. The sound of heavy panting comes from the left. It is hard for Kate to compute what she observes in the nearby clearing. Nathanial's mangled body is prone and mostly covered with autumn leaves and dirt. The seat of his plaid golf pants has been ripped away. His left buttock is missing. Pelvic bone is exposed. A yard away is Nathanael's chewed arm.

Kate is frozen in horror. The bear lumbers into view. Strands of pink drool dangles from its mouth. The tip of one of its fangs has chipped off. It sniffs her scent. Soil and gore are caked on the bear's nose and black fur. A glint of orange and red flashes in the animal's eyes.

The entity hisses, "Thy will be done!"

Kate manages to scream. The bear charges and goes straight for her womb. Not even an unborn Dudley is to be spared.

Little People's Village

Connecticut Extreme Horror

A. Sanford

A beer can sails through the night air and explodes against a tree trunk with an ejaculation of suds. The sweet stink of cannabis broadcasts on curls of smoke. Rowdy laughter and teenage voices

echo in the dark forest.

"Keep it down! The cops will come," Zoe warns.

"Fuck the police!" Mario shouts. He takes a swig of Bacardi straight from the bottle and coughs. The front of his football jersey is wet with 151.

Kyle stumbles about, appearing bulky in his camouflage hunting jacket. He bangs his shin on a small brick structure cemented in the ground. Shitfaced, he falls forward.

Mario roars in amusement, "Dude, you just took a header over a doll house!"

Sitting up and rubbing his leg, Kyle yells back, "Who built a fuckin' brick doll house in the middle of the fuckin' woods?" He then kicks at the edifice with his steel-toed work boot. A piece of the mortar chips off.

"Don't break it!" Zoe scolds, "It's an artifact." "An art-ah what?" slurs Kyle.

"Geek alert. Don't ask her to explain." Mario mocks.

Close by, Samantha is wandering about in the bright moonlight. She is wearing a Peruvian knitted hat with colorful pompoms. Samantha heartens, "Isn't this place so interesting at night! Look, there's another miniature house over there. I hope to see one of the little people that live inside. They're supposed to be fairies. Anybody believe in fairies?"

Mario jokes, "Kyle's a fairy."

"Fuck you, faggot!" Kyle barks at his friend.

Samantha rolls her eyes. "Really mature. Will you two guys ever grow up?" She then stops and addresses Zoe. "Hey, so nice that you came to hang out. I really liked your pottery in the school art exhibit this year."

Blushing, Zoe replies, "Oh, it wasn't that good." She nervously tugs the drawstring on her black hoody.

"Yes it was," Samantha smiles. "You're really talented. You should go to art school in like, New York or Paris, or any place that's awesome."

"I wish," Zoe sighs. "Gotta stay around here." "How come?"

Embarrassed, Zoe answers, "I have to help my mom take care of my brother. Eddy's a handful."

"Your brother Eddy is a fuckin' weirdo," said Mario. "Don't be so mean," Samantha huffs.

"He's autistic," Zoe says.

"I don't care," Mario grumbles. "I'll still beat his retarded ass again when I see him."

Kyle gloats, "I once put Eddy in a jujitsu sleeper-hold and choked him out. He pissed his pants. When he came to, he balled his eyes out and had a seizure."

Mario gives Kyle a high-five and bellows, "Nice!"

Samantha senses that Zoe is about to cry and takes her under the arm. She quickly mutters, "Let's get way from these two assholes. Do you see the fairy king's chair over there?" Samantha points to a clearing among the trees.

Nearby, in an alcove, a seat of stone has been fashioned into the embankment. The blocks of granite are crudely cut. Crumbling rust-colored cement makes up the backrest. In descending order, an aperture, triangle and circle are carved into the old mortar. The Kennedy twins are taking turns sitting in the seat while Bridget from the high school yearbook is snapping photos. Stark flashes illuminate the scene.

A bit baked, Greg passes by Samantha and Zoe.

Samantha calls out to Greg, "Did you sit in the fairy king's seat yet? It's suppose to bring you good luck."

Greg nods, "Yup." The whites of his eyes are pink slits. "Are you leaving?" Samantha asks.

"Yeah," Greg replies. "Have to pickup my little sister."

"Ah, too bad," pouts Samantha. Samantha then turns to Zoe and whispers in her ear, "I am so in love with him. God, is he cute!"

A short distance away in the shadows, nobody notices that Rebecca has passed out and is laying in a mound of decaying autumn leaves. She has no jacket. All she is wearing is a Nirvana tee shirt and ripped bellbottoms. Rebecca had drunk a full bottle of Zinfandel and popped two of her mother's Xanax. One of the tiny houses is in close proximity to her body. Standing only a few feet high, the structure's miniature front door and little windows are clogged with spider webs, acorns, and fragments of chipmunk bones.

"We got accepted to Storrs!" announces one of the Kennedy twins. The twins are wearing identical UCONN Husky sweatshirts.

"Congratulations!" Samantha cheers.

The twins get up to allow Samantha to have a seat. Bridget takes another blinding flash.

"Come on, Zoe, you're next," Samantha encourages.

Zoe is not used to the attention from her classmates. A surge of anxiety makes her pulse race. Feeling lightheaded, she lowers herself down onto the stone chair.

"Say cheese!" says Bridget as she snaps the photo.

Zoe cringes and shuts her eyes. At that very moment, a sodomizing current arises from the seat and penetrates through the girl's blue jeans. The violating sensation travels up Zoe's spinal cord and into her brain like an electrical shock. It quickly dissipates but leaves Zoe trembling and nauseous. She vomits a geyser of Peach Snapple and granola.

"Eww!" one of the Kennedy twins grimaces.

Samantha rushes forward to help Zoe up from the stone chair. "Are you okay?"

Wobbly, Zoe hangs on to Samantha and groans, "I don't feel good."

"Did you drink too much?" "No."

"What happened?" "Not sure."

"You're really shivering."

"I'm kinda scared," Zoe whimpers. "I think I better go home." Mortified, she uses her sleeve to wipe the puke off her chin.

A Kennedy twin whines, "Why is it so cold all of a sudden?"

Reflexively clutching herself, Bridget chimes in, "Well, we can wrap this up. I took enough pictures for the yearbook spread."

Samantha supports Zoe around the waist. "Come on babe, I got you. Let's walk."

One of the Kennedy twins switches on a flashlight. A jiggling beam shines down the dirt trail which is aligned with black forest and overhanging tree limbs. Together, the five girls begin to depart.

"Hey, why are all you bitches taking off?" shouts Mario. "I thought we were supposed to take a group photo!"

Bridget flips Mario the bird. Nearby, Kyle is trying to steady himself as he urinates. A stream of piss splatters on the little weird house that he tripped over.

A Kennedy twin sneers, "Those boys are such creeps."

Mario takes another gulp of Bacardi and hollers at his classmates, "Okay, leave then! I don't care. All of you are just a bunch of stuck-up dykes anyway!"

The five girls hurry their pace and continue toward the main road.

Angry and cocked, Mario walks over to the stone chair. He plops down in a huff. Inebriated, he is oblivious to the drop in temperature. Kyle comes stumbling forward to find Mario. He falls again. Writhing for a moment in a pile of dead leaves, Kyle touches a pale thin human arm.

"Wow, I just tripped over a body!" Kyle gasps.

Mario calls out to Kyle in the darkness, "Dude, where are you?" He hears Kyle straining and mumbling. Soon, Mario sees the shape of Kyle and someone else in a patch of moonlight. His drunk friend is attempting to carry a girl over his shoulder.

"Who the fuck is that?" Mario blurts.

Excited and wheezing, Kyle says, "It's-It's Rebecca. She's passed out!"

Mario takes another quick swig of rum and stands up. Kyle almost drops the girl as he struggles toward the stone chair.

"Sit her down!" orders Mario.

Clumsily, Kyle lets Rebecca fall like he was dumping a sack of garbage. The listless girl's head whacks against the old mortar. She moans but does not wake.

"Man, she is totally out of it!" said Mario.

Breathing heavily, Kyle says, "When I found her, I thought she OD'd or something."

"Well, she's alive alright."

Rebecca's skin is the color of porcelain in ambient lunar glow.

Kyle takes a hard swallow and pants, "Damn, she's pretty."
"What do we do now?" Mario asks anxiously.

"She looks really cold," Kyle says with a dirty smile.

There is a tense pause. Through the dim of night, both boys have glints of fervor in their eyes. The deviant grin grows broader on Kyle's face as he lowers his voice and slurs, "M-M-Maybe I should sit her in my lap and give her a n-n--nice hug to keep her warm."

Amped and nervous, Mario goes to guzzle the Bacardi but the bottle slips from his hand. It hits the ground and shatters on a hunk of crumbling mortar. "Damn it!" Mario curses. Rum soaks into the earth.

A short distance away, something little darts out from one of the miniatures houses. Then a second one scampers into the open. And another. And another. Rustling about in the dead autumn leaves, they become a clandestine audience.

***

Middlebury, Connecticut
Nearly seven years later

It is a grey afternoon in October. Light is fading. Dead autumn leaves scatter about as the black Infiniti coup rolls down the street. The upscale neighborhood is aligned with newly constructed Mc-Mansions. Conspicuously, the vehicle comes to an abrupt stop at the end of a cul-de-sac. Mario has a .380 LCP tucked in his belt. In the trunk of the sports car, he has a Glock model 17 loaded with an illegal high capacity magazine. A premonition tells him to bring along the 9mm but he does not want to imprint through his leather jacket. Lowering the brim of his Ecko cap to hide his face, Mario hurriedly exits the Infiniti. He proceeds up a brick walkway toward the last residence on the left. In an upstairs window of the house, the curtain moves as someone watches Mario approach the front entrance. Down below, before Mario can knock, the door opens.

"Quick, get inside!" Samantha says with a hushed voice.

"Who's that spyin' on me from the upstairs window?" Mario

snarls as he steps into the foyer. "Is this a setup? If it is, you'll be fuckin' sorry."

Samantha slams the door shut and locks it. She then reactivates the alarm.

It has been nearly seven years. Mario notices that Samantha is no longer the hippie vegan girl he knew in high school. She is now preppy, proper and dressed in a Talbot's pants suit.

"Are ya gonna tell me what the fuck this is all about?" Mario demands.

"Yes. Go sit in the living room!" snaps Samantha. There are tears in her eyes.

Mario has also morphed with time. He is short but jacked with roid-induced muscles. Having left richie-rich Middlebury, Mario opened a car wash in West Haven with a cousin. The business is used for laundering drug money. Heroin and PCP are the main products they sling.

In the well appointed living room, Zoe sits in the middle of an expensive beige couch. Dressed in over-stretched frumpy blue sweats, she has gained seventy pounds due to years of emotional eating. Zoe cringes as Mario walks in.

Mario jeers with a nasty grin, "Wow, looks like somebody needs a gastric by-pass! I see ya have been hittin' the buffets hard since graduation."

Zoe does her best not to cry. "Sit down!" Samantha orders.

Mario snaps back at Samantha, "Tell me who's upstairs or I'm leavin'!"

Nervously, Zoe answers, "It's Eddy. He's upstairs playing video games."

Surprised, Mario looks back at Zoe. "Eddy, your retard of a brother?"

Zoe replies, "My mom died. I'm his caregiver. He's with me 24/7."

Samantha states sternly, "Eddy can't hear any of this. He's not to be involved."

"Any of what?" Mario barks.

"Take a seat and we'll discuss what's going on," says Samantha.

Reluctantly, Mario sits down into a chair. He quickly scans around the spacious living room. Squinting, he asks Samantha, "So, is this your house? Pretty nice crib."

"It's my parent's home. They're down in Florida right now." "I get it; you're another spoiled Middlebury girl still livin' with wealthy mommy and daddy."

Samantha glares back at Mario. "I see that you're still a bully."

Mario shoots a quick look over at Zoe and inquires with a sarcastic smirk, "Are you two an item? One lipstick, one butch." "No, we haven't talked in years," responds Samantha with mounting anger in her voice.

"Okay why the reunion? I wasn't sure if all your urgent text messages weren't a fuckin' prank."

Samantha says, "Do you remember Rebecca?"

The malicious smirk disappears from Mario's face. He pauses. Then lies, "No."

Samantha says bitterly, "Well, she remembered you. She

mentioned you and Kyle in a ME TOO post."

Mario stiffens in his seat. "What the hell are ya talkin' about?"

Zoe whimpers, "Rebecca committed suicide last week. She hung herself. It was in the local newspaper."

"What happened at Little People's Village?" says Samantha with fury in her eyes. "What did you two do to her?"

"Nothin'! I don't remember! Are you tryin' to get me in trouble?" Mario's skin is starting to redden.

Tears roll down Zoe's cheeks. "That night, we thought she left early. We would have never left her behind."

"What are ya accusin' me of? We were drunk! I don't recall shit! She was an emo-goth chick that was into cuttin'. Rebecca was always a flake. I'm not surprised she off'ed herself."

"So you're lying; you do remember her!" Samantha points her finger at Mario's face.

Mario yells back at Samantha, "Is this some sort of shake-down? Extortion game!"

"No! We have something else to warn you about." "What?"

"Did you sit in the fairy king's throne?" "Huh?"

"Answer me! Did you sit in that stone seat in the woods?" "What? I don't know what the fuck you are talkin' about! I'm not admittin' to one goddamn thing'!" Anxiously, Mario plays with the keys in his jacket pocket and unintentionally presses the remote. He does not hear the chirp of the car alarm being deactivated. The Infiniti's trunk is popped open by the key fob.

Samantha addresses Zoe, "Tell him what you told me."

Zoe takes another deep breath and states, "As kids we

thought, that sitting in the fairy king's throne would bring us good luck. But it can also be a curse. At certain times in the solstice, entities from a different dimension appear and can caste judgment on mankind. They can be merciless."

Starting to tremble, Samantha says, "This is the anniversary of all of us being at Little People's Village. If the fairies are upset, all that sat in the throne will be annihilated within seven years. At midnight it will be exactly seven years. It is possible that we will die in a few hours. "

Mario abruptly bursts out laughing, "Holy shit! I am being punked! You two can't be fuckin' serious? Little People's Village is just part of an old amusement park. Everybody knows that them little doll houses were part of a stupid carnival attraction for kids."

Samantha balls up her hands and tries to maintain a rationale tone. "At first, I didn't believe this either. But look what has happened so far. I was supposed to marry Greg but he got killed by an IED in Mosul. He sat in the seat. Brenda died of an aneurysm at age 21. Both Kennedy twins went down in a private plane crash a day after graduation from UCONN. They all sat in the seat. What happened to your friend Kyle?"

Taken aback, Mario replies, "Listen, everybody is croakin' from opiates every minute in this freakin' country! He OD'd last summer. But it was Fentanyl not fuckin' fairies that killed him!"

"Don't you think it is strange that so many of our classmates died?"

Mario shakes his head in frustration, "No, it's all a fuckin' coincidence! Weird shit happens all the time. People die in all fuckin' kinds of ways. Somebody just got hacked to pieces in Milford. Did ya hear about the couple that got eaten by a bear in Cornwall? I don't believe in curses, ghosts, aliens, Big Foot--none of that bullshit!"

Zoe exhales and says with conviction, "I'm Wiccan and I have been studying the paranormal world for some time now. Entities sometimes choose abandoned places to manifest and cause havoc. They hide in the folklore and fables. The entities can be wicked and relish in the fact that their victims will not be believed. The victims are abused and not taken seriously by society. The victims are considered crazy. The victims are considered to be making things up."

Mario responds, "Tryin' to fuckin' trick me up with this superstitious angle, aren't ya? You're not gettin' me to confess!"

Zoe says, "Samantha and I wanted you to come here and take part in a seance. We are the last three survivors of the curse. I was hoping we could join hands tonight and petition the entities for forgiveness. Maybe we will be pardoned."

Mario bolts up from his seat and says irately, "Holy shit, you cunts are really fuckin' nuts! I am out of here!"

"Please don't go!" Samantha shouts.

Mario heads to the foyer. For a split second, he glances to his left and feels a damp breeze. Down a hallway, near a second set of stairs, the sliders are open to the backyard. Samantha in her haste had failed to set the alarm for that zone. Making it to the inner front entrance, Mario grabs the knob and yanks open the door. Eddy is standing outside on the stoop. He is 6'1, bone-thin and emaciated.

Clad in nerd wear, Eddy has on a Star Wars' tee shirt, khaki trousers and Converse high-tops. His wild blue eyes are bulging as he points the firearm. Eddy had retrieved Mario's Glock from the trunk of the Infiniti. In a sudden panic, Mario has no time to draw the .380 stowed in his waistband. Reflexively, he screams, "DON'T!" puts up his hand and is shot through the palm. The 9mm hollow point travels on and enters Mario's thick muscular neck, nicking his trachea. Mario clutches his throat and wheezes with a high pitched whistle. There is the blended sensation of searing pain and asphyxiation. Mario spins around and drops to his knees in the foyer. Shiny brass shell casings eject and tumble as Eddy shoots Mario two more times in the upper back. The sharp popping reports mixes with the beeping alarm chime. Eddy continues into the house and encounters Samantha.

"Eddy please no!" Samantha screams.

In the next second, Samantha's blonde hair flips up as a round penetrates the top of her cranium. Three more rapid shots zip over her head, pock the wall and shatter a decorative mirror. She falls to the carpet. Eddy leans down and places the muzzle of the Glock to Samantha's chest and fires once. Point blank contact produces a blackened star-shaped wound. He continues on into the living room.

Zoe does not attempt to rise from the couch. In her final moment of despair, she is aware that the entities have hijacked her brother's will. She knows that the entities are not righteous in their wrath.

Her last utterance is, "Unjust and indiscriminate."

The 9mm hollow point mushrooms and rips a dime sized hole in Zoe's pounding heart.

There are ten more shots left in the gun. Eddy robotically returns to his first victim. Mario is still conscious and squirming on his belly. A pink froth is bubbling out of his mouth. His eyes are wide with terror. He tries to verbally plead but can only gurgle as he chokes on his own blood. In an ear-splitting folly, Eddy empties the remaining bullets toward Mario's head. Some of the rounds miss and fragment a couple of floor tiles. Some hit Mario's skull, blowing off his Ecko cap and eliciting a momentary pink mist. The slide to the Glock model 17 locks back signaling that the gun is now empty. Hot spent shell casings are rolling about the foyer. Mario is motionless as a dark pool is spreading from under his body. The occipital portion of his skull is misshapen and leaking fatty brain matter from a fissure.

Eddy sniffs the air and smells burnt propellant, urine and shit.

His sneakers and khaki trousers are speckled red. His hearing is temporary impaired due to the 17 gun shots. The house alarm is blaring. Samantha is unconscious and on the verge of death. The sound of her sucking chest wound is not discernable. Zoe is slumped in the middle of the living room couch like a large dead Buddha. Eddy tosses the Glock. Again, he exits through the sliders. In the backyard, Eddy pauses to remove his Converse High Tops and rainbow socks. Barefooted, he flees into the woods. There are the sounds of approaching sirens.

I-84, Connecticut

As dawn rises, an elderly Dominican woman is the first to witness the abomination as she peers out the top floor window at the senior housing complex. Next, is a prostitute on the street, working in the morning for some crack-cocaine. The hooker looks up for a moment thinks she's trippin'. Next, a trucker on I-84 slams on his breaks and can't believe what he is seeing. High on a peak, overlooking the city, the iconic 50 foot cross has been inverted. The laws of physics have been broken. The inversion occurred in the passing of a nanosecond. Eddy is standing at the base of the upside down cross. Most of the skin is missing from the soles of his bleeding feet. During the night, he made the pilgrimage from Middlebury, through the woods and alongside the interstate. Eddy was barefoot the entire way. Many times police cars zoomed by Eddy but he was undetected. The entities shrouded his passage.

There are more sounds of sirens. I-84 is backing up. Eddy turns and genuflects in front of the massive icon. The hissing entities in his brain lied and told him he would be bestowed with special gifts for doing their will.

Eddy beams with a religious-like ecstasy. He announces aloud with a giant smile, "I even shot my own fatso sister for you. Time for my rewards."

There is a pause of silence in his mind. Abruptly, the entities have ceased their hissing and chattering.

"Give me super powers," Eddy requests.

The entities then start to laugh at Eddy in a frenzied chorus.

Eddy instantly is racked with all-consuming dread. He starts to shake and convulse. A dark piss stain is growing in the crotch of his khaki trousers. A current of devastating energy emits from the cross. In the next moment, Eddy is pulverized like a gnat before a colossal bug-zapper. Chunks of his carbonized skeleton scatter across the ground and smolder.

Down below on the streets of the city, many think the inversion of the cross is some sort of elaborate Halloween hoax. The old Dominican woman clutches her crucifix and mutters in Spanish, "El apocalipsis."

www.ingramcontent.com/pod-product-compliance
Lightning Source LLC
Chambersburg PA
CBHW071513150726
48000CB00002B/571